AN ISLAND CHRISTMAS

A WINTRY TALE OF LOVE, FAMILY AND IMPOSSIBLE CHOICES

HELENA HALME

COPYRIGHT

For Dad

FOREWORD

The Åland islands lie in the waters between Finland and Sweden. Although a self-governing region of Finland, the group of 6,700 islands, of which only 60 are inhabited, remain exclusively Swedish-speaking.

The quirkiness of the islanders is often attributed to their rich history. Due to its strategic location, there have been many wars and would-be invaders. Swedes, Russians, the French, and the British have fought on these shores.

A small seafaring nation, the Åland islands have a distinct culture of their own, forged over years of hardship and perseverance. The people living on these rocky outcrops and on the main island around the capital Mariehamn, have a deep sense of independence and identity. If you ask an islander whether he feels Swedish or Finnish, the reply will always be, 'Neither. I'm an *Ålänning.'*

Due to its tax-free status, Åland is today dominated by

tourism and ferry traffic. Several popular cruise liners stop in Mariehamn to take advantage of the discounted food, alcohol, and other consumer goods, bringing in day-trippers to the islands. The ferries and people in this story are fictional, although based on empirical research.

ONE

On Alicia's first winter back home, snow arrives late on the Åland islands. It's the last weekend before Christmas and finally, overnight, a heavy fall covers everything with a pure white blanket. Alicia loves the dramatically altered scenery of the islands, when the sea is frozen over and the teal color of the shipping lanes by the West Harbor is highlighted by the brilliant landscape. Gone are the dull brown fields and the gray buildings, made even more drab by the wind and rain that are the theme of fall.

As she sits in her mother's kitchen, drinking a hot cup of coffee, surveying the coastal view through the window, she smiles to herself. The virgin layer of snow makes the distant sea seem like an extension of the white fields, drawing a straight line between the ice and the blue skies above. It's as if the weather gods have heard her prayers and granted her greatest wish.

This Christmas, her first on the islands since she made a surprise move back to her home six months ago, is going to be perfect. Not only is it her first Christmas here in at least ten years, but it is also her granddaughter's very first Yuletide. How she looks forward to seeing what the little girl will make of the traditional Christmas tree, lit with real candles, at her great-grandmother's house.

Alicia remembers when her son, Stefan, saw the tree, as tall as the room, for the first time. It was Christmas Eve and they were about to sit down for their midday porridge, another tradition her mother, Hilda, insisted on. Stefan, just turned one, had clapped his hands and uttered his first word, *"Ljus"—candle*—in Swedish. He had said the word with such clarity that it had brought tears of joy into Hilda's eyes. The candles on the tree were lit just twice each day of the holidays, once for lunch and once for dinner. Uffe had the task of going around the branches, carefully bringing a match to each candle, while making sure the old candleholders were securely clamped onto a thick branch, and that there was enough space above the flame.

Alicia's thoughts turn to her granddaughter. She thinks of little Anne Sofie as a wonderful surprise gift awarded to her nearly four months ago, when life hadn't seemed worth living. Each breath she took during that dark period had been weighed down by the memory of how her son had perished in a motorcycle accident back in London. She had felt so abandoned and lonely, until she returned to the islands.

And met Patrick.

Alicia thinks of England, where she had lived for nearly twenty years. She remembers what pandemonium a heavy snowfall caused. London would stop in its tracks and everyone would be amazed by this strange natural phenomenon. During all the time Alicia lived in England, there had been at least one chaotic snow day every year. She always marveled at the surprise on people's faces when buses didn't run or trains froze to a standstill.

'This happens to you every time!' she wanted to shout, but of course she didn't. She was a good immigrant, always conforming, always modifying her behavior to the customs of her adopted country.

She took another sip of the hot, warming liquid. How liberating it was not to have to bite her tongue anymore. Or worry that she'd said the wrong thing, or hadn't understood some veiled criticism.

It took Alicia years to get used to living in the UK. She'd been so in love with Liam that nothing—not even her struggles to adapt to her new country—stopped her from wanting to be with him. And then, of course, when Stefan was born, she slowly began to feel at home in London. Alicia shakes her head to banish the dull ache and sadness that overwhelms her each time she thinks of her lovely boy, who didn't get to see his eighteenth birthday. Instead, she turns her thoughts to Anne Sofie, her new grandchild. She finds her phone and looks at the latest picture Frida, Stefan's girlfriend and the baby's mother, has posted on their private online app. The little girl is the most beautiful baby Alicia has ever seen. But she would think that, wouldn't she?

When Frida had dropped the bombshell of her pregnancy in the summer, it had taken Alicia—and especially Liam—quite a while to get used to the idea that their dead 17-year-old son had fathered a child. But when Alicia saw the baby in Frida's arms in the hospital a few weeks later, she wasn't prepared for the absolute love she felt for the new little person. She hadn't expected the joy she experienced at Frida's bedside. When she held Anne Sofie, she sensed a connection like no other. It wasn't the overwhelming adoration mingled with a massive weight of responsibility that she had felt when she first held Stefan. No, this was something much purer, much simpler, and far, far more enjoyable. The first time she saw her little granddaughter, with her eyes firmly shut and her little rosy mouth making sucking noises, searching for her mother's breast, the tiny amount of doubt that Alicia still carried about the baby's paternity disappeared like a puff of smoke.

Alicia is shaken out of her thoughts by the arrival of Patrick. He's standing at the front door wearing a shiny, thick padded coat. Alicia spots the round Moncler logo on the sleeve and smiles. The divorce from Mia Eriksson hasn't altered his shopping habits, it seems. He's stamping his boots against the thick mat that Hilda has placed at the front door for just such a purpose.

'At your service,' he says, grinning.

'Coffee before you start?' Alicia says.

'That'd be nice. Any of Hilda's cinnamon buns going?'

He takes off his boots and jacket.

Alicia shakes her head and laughs. 'I'll have a look. I bet she made a batch before they left.'

She finds them neatly bagged in the freezer and takes two sweet buns out and puts them in the oven.

'So, how are you?' Patrick says. He's standing on the

other side of the kitchen island, a safe distance from Alicia. This is the routine they have settled on. No touching, no closeness, and definitely no flirting.

'It's very kind of you to offer to shift the snow. I'm so out of practice, I don't think I'd know where to start.'

Last night, the snow didn't stop falling and the lane has a thick layer over it. Alicia's car is safely in the barn, which Hilda and Uffe use as a garage. She's not sure what she would have done if Patrick hadn't responded to her message earlier that morning and agreed to come and help.

Patrick shrugs his wide shoulders. He's wearing a bottle-green jumper with a zip at the collar. Somehow the color makes his blue eyes more intense, or perhaps it's the ruddiness of his cheeks, caused by the chill outside.

'Mia is in Stockholm with the girls, so I have a free weekend.'

'Even so, I'm grateful. Hilda and Uffe are coming back on the morning sailing, so they'll be here at 3pm at the latest. I don't want Uffe to have to start digging his way into the house as soon as he's home from sunny Spain.'

Alicia hears the ping from the oven and turns around. She can feel the heat of his body even with a solid piece of kitchen furniture between them. It's the intense gaze in those damn eyes of his.

Why did I accept his offer to help with the snow? Did I really think I was over him? Stupid, stupid woman.

After taking the tractor fitted with a snow plow up and

down the lane to Uffe and Hilda's house, Patrick comes back in, his boots clattering in the hallway. Alicia has decided to offer him lunch, it's the least she can do to repay him for the favor. She tries to convince herself that this is the reason, but she knows she wants to extend the time she spends with him outside of their work.

'Would you like something to eat?' she asks when he sits down on one of the kitchen chairs.

Patrick looks up, surprised.

'Or at least a beer? You must be tired after all that physical exercise?'

His ruddy face looks even more attractive, if possible, and Alicia has to turn her eyes away from him.

'Beer would be great,' Patrick says. He lifts his eyes up to her and adds, 'Look, Alicia, I'm really glad to help you out, but I wanted to talk to you.'

'Sandwiches OK?' Alicia interrupts him. She doesn't want to have this conversation now. She still doesn't know how she feels.

Patrick sighs. 'OK,' he replies simply.

TWO

Brit gazes at the ship as she waits for one of the car deck guys to open the gate. The vast ferry looks almost threatening. The bow, as yet empty of vehicles, is agape, resembling the mouth of a huge whale or a fantastical monster. Staring at the large red Marie Line logo on the hull, she wonders if she has made a mistake. Why didn't she choose the Caribbean cruise she'd been offered instead of hankering after Christmas at home? She'd told herself she would miss the cold and the snow. It looked like God had answered her prayers a little too enthusiastically: there was a snow storm brewing. A lot of the white stuff had already fallen. Brit can't remember a December like it. Apart from the shipping lane, a channel of dark water, the sea is covered with ice. A faint sun plays on the surface, making it glint as if it is covered with small precious stones. Involuntarily, Brit touches the ring finger of her left hand with her thumb. She needs to be honest with herself. She's on the run, fleeing a bad relationship, plain and simple. She shakes her head. She's done with men for the foreseeable future. She's going to make the best of this job, whatever. Working on the Stockholm ferries may be a step back from her managerial job with Royal Caribbean, but at least here she will be able to visit her father on the islands more often.

It's 7am and Brit shivers. She is cold in spite of the warm padded coat she'd bought at NK as soon as she got back. She realizes her new gloves are in one of the boxes stacked in the car. This, her 10-year-old red VW Golf, which has been waiting for her patiently at a garage in Stockholm, contains the whole of her life. During the week spent in an Airbnb near Slussen, now a trendy area in southern Stockholm, she'd gone through the storage unit she'd rented since she began working on the cruisers twenty years ago. Many times during the long hours spent sifting through her old books, photographs, and the silly ornaments she'd collected on her travels to ports around the world, she'd been tempted to just sit on the cold floor of the unit and weep. Weep for the kitchen table and chairs she'd kept in the expectation that she and Nico would one day settle down and have a home, and even perhaps a family.

Don't think about The Rat!

Brit glances at the ship again. Her new career onboard MS *Sabrina* seems an utterly foolish idea now. She'd worked on the ferries between Finland and Sweden in her youth, but she'd been in her teens then, not in her late thirties, with failure already etched onto her face.

Now, as one of the more senior members of the Marie Line crew, it was a different proposition altogether.

Not just a summer job that she can take or leave. She would have to make this new position a success. And why wouldn't she? Just because she'd had to flee her old job on account of the bastard she thought she would spend the rest of her life with, didn't mean she was a failure, did it? Brit would show him, show everybody, all his friends (and some of hers), that she was strong and could manage on her own.

Feeling desperately nervous about the prospect of meeting her new colleagues on the monster of a ferry in front of her, Brit glances at her face in the rear-view mirror. She checks there's no lipstick on her teeth and puffs up her hair with her fingers. Pushing the mirror down, she lifts her chin up and gives the old guy in the bright orange vest who's waving her into the belly of the ship a wide smile.

Jukka likes to come onto the bridge well before they are due to sail, when it's still empty. After an overnight docking in Stockholm, this morning MS *Sabrina* would be heading back to Helsinki in Finland across Ålands Hav via Mariehamn, where most of the day-trippers would change ferries. Jukka doesn't expect a difficult sailing. The shipping lanes have been cleared and although the passengers will no doubt be in festive mood so close to Christmas, the ferry is only about three-quarters full.

As he checks the monitors to the decks below him, to make sure the staff are getting into position by the open bow doors, he sees a good-looking woman step out of a red Golf on the car deck area reserved for employees. For a fraction of a second, he thinks she looks directly at him. But she can't know about the cameras at the side of the deck. Or can she?

Jukka sees she has a good figure, her shapely curves hugged by a tight skirt and boots with high heels, visible under an open padded coat. Her hair is long and dark and her face looks friendly, but her expression appears vulnerable. Jukka follows the woman as she pulls a suitcase toward the bow of the ship. He sighs as she disappears inside.

He shakes his head and tells himself to concentrate on the task in hand, yet he can't help wonder who the woman is. After he's made the regulatory checks, and seen that the car deck is populated by the correct number of crew, Jukka allows himself a glance at the staffing sheets. And there it is. A new restaurant manager is starting onboard today. 'Britt Svensson,' he reads out loud, deciding that he needs to go and say hello to the woman. It's his duty as Captain of the ship after all. There's nothing else to it, just business and professionalism, Jukka tells himself as he makes his way to his cabin.

Brit is shown around the staff quarters by an older woman, who says she's the assistant restaurant manager, 'Or acting manager until today.' She introduces herself as Kerstin Eklund. Brit glances at her uniform and sees there are two stripes at the cuffs. Kerstin has a few years on Brit, with a thin, wiry frame and short brown hair. She has a long face with very narrow lips painted bright red, and Brit longs to tell her that some of the lipstick has run at the side of her mouth, but is unsure if she should. Perhaps later, after she has officially met all of her staff, she can take Kerstin to one side and point it out. Brit is so preoccupied by Kerstin's lipstick that she doesn't notice a tall man with light brown hair, who stands in front of her as they step inside the passenger area of the ship.

'Welcome onboard MS *Sabrina*!' Jukka cringes inwardly at the cliché. Kerstin gives him a look that says, *I know your game.* Why does he always feel so intimidated by the older, female, members of the crew?

'Thank you Kerstin, I can take it from here,' he says, trying to sound authoritative.

The woman nods and scuttles along the corridor toward the staff quarters. He should have reminded her that, as acting restaurant manager, it was still her job to make sure the bar was fully stocked, and that the staff had gathered to welcome the new manager, but he lets it pass. Glancing at his watch he sees that there is more than half an hour until boarding begins. Plenty of time to go through the motions. He turns toward Brit Svensson.

'I'm Jukka Markusson, the Captain.'

The woman smiles, nodding at his uniform. 'I gathered that.'

This makes Jukka cough. The woman is even more good-looking at close hand. She's got striking green eyes, and her dark hair has a chestnut tinge to it. Briefly, he wonders if she is wearing colored contact lenses and whether she has dyed her hair, but then realizes how inappropriate his thoughts are.

Be professional.

It was his infatuation with a woman onboard that nearly cost him his career a few years back, something which the older members of the crew, particularly Kerstin, never let him forget. Although no one actually mentions the affair anymore–at least not in front of him.

'You've met Kerstin, the acting manager. She will show you the ropes during this first passage to Helsinki. Then, for the return leg, you can take over. As you know, we will dock at Mariehamn at 14.10, and sail onward to Finland proper when the island passengers and day-trippers have disembarked,' Here Jukka glances at his list, which shows that the majority of the passengers would leave the ship. He knows that most of the passengers on these cruises are blind drunk by the time they disembark in Mariehamn. Same goes for those who come onboard from the sister ferry to *Sabrina*.

He tries not to get involved in the messy antics of the Finns and Swedes onboard, but he is sometimes called to attend to the more serious incidents, such as fights, or an injury caused by drunken brawling between young men. These days, women also get themselves embroiled in dangerous cat fights. Once, he had to confiscate a knuckleduster from a 16-year-old girl who'd used it to cut the face of another teenager. Both looked as if butter wouldn't melt when Jukka handed them over to the police in Helsinki Harbor.

The most serious incident of all was a man overboard. When a snowstorm was pending, as it was today, with chill winds and the temperature of the sea barely above freezing, anyone falling into the shipping lane would lose their life instantly. And most probably never be found.

But he's used to dealing with drunks. At least he's more at home in his role as the ship's policeman than he is as the head of staff, most of whom are female.

Jukka lifts his gaze toward the woman, who is looking at him attentively.

Goodness, those eyes really are something else.

Jukka coughs again in an effort to keep his thoughts from wandering.

'This time of the year, we will be able to depart Mariehamn within fifteen minutes. We only have just over 800 passengers onboard today. Our ETA in Helsinki is 19.50. The restaurant and bars will be busy this close to Christmas, so you should be vigilant for any trouble. You will be on call for the whole of the journey. Any questions?'

The woman smiles again. She has a knowing expression on her face and Jukka wonders if Kerstin has already spilled the beans about his old misadventure. He straightens his back and corrects his cap.

Brit doesn't say anything, just gazes at him, the smile reaching all the way into those green eyes, and making his heart beat even harder against his uniform.

THREE

W hile she waits for Uffe and Hilda's car to appear in the lane, Alicia is once again alone in the kitchen of their large house. She's been housesitting during her mother and stepfather's two-week holiday. Not that there is any chance of a burglary being committed–she can't remember when such a thing last happened on the islands, if it ever had. For some reason, however, Hilda is convinced that something will happen to the three-story building if is left empty.

The light has begun to fade already, although the snow makes the landscape appear more luminous. The skies are clear too and after the faint winter sunshine of the day, the horizon is lit with reds and oranges. Alicia wonders why she ever wished to leave this place. But in her teens she had felt stranded on these islands, cut off from the real world. Now being isolated seems more attractive, but more than that, Alicia feels a sense of belonging that she never felt in England. She's not prepared to give that up.

Her thoughts turn to Liam, who is due to arrive two days before Christmas. He's been taking more time off from his busy surgery schedule lately. How, Alicia can't fathom. During their last Skype call, he'd said he had *some significant news*.

Alicia has gone back to their house in London only once since her surprise move to the islands. She spent a week doing things that she can't do over the internet, like seeing her doctor and dentist. She will handle all those things here, on the islands, as soon as she and Liam have decided what to do about the house and their marriage. She expected the trip back to London to be more emotional, but it seemed, in her mind, she had already moved back home to Åland. Toward the end of the trip, she was counting the days and hours until she would be back on the Marie Line ferry, crossing the Ålands Hav from Stockholm to the islands.

'Have you lost weight?' Hilda says as soon as she's given Alicia a hug. 'You're just skin and bones!'

'Hello to you too,' Alicia says, glancing at Uffe, who winks at her. 'Did you have a nice time?'

Her mother is wearing a pair of red kitten-heel boots, most unsuitable for the weather. They both look tanned, although there is a slightly worried, harassed air about Hilda.

'Are you OK?' Alicia asks her mother.

'Not really! We nearly had an accident by the swing bridge,' she says, sitting down.

'Didn't we?' She addresses this to Uffe, who's looking down at his hands. He's seated at the kitchen table while Alicia perches on her favorite stool by the window. Eventually Uffe nods, and so her mother turns toward Alicia and carries on talking, barely drawing breath.

'A Russian, in one of those enormous Jeeps, they're called Cherokee, or something aren't they?'

Alicia knows nothing about cars, but she replies. 'Yes, I think so. But what happened?'

Alicia glances over to Uffe to see if he can make sense of what her mother is saying, but her stepfather has his head bent, his eyes firmly set on his hands, which hang between his legs.

'Well, he nearly rammed us over!' Hilda says, her voice rising. There's panic in her red-rimmed eyes. On close inspection, there's something new in her mother's demeanor. Perhaps she had one too many glasses of wine on the flight back from Alicante.

At Hilda's outburst, Uffe gets up. Before turning to go out of the door, he says quietly, 'It was nothing. He was just trying to overtake us, wanting to get to the bridge before it goes up.'

Alicia watches her mother purse her lips, but she doesn't contradict her husband. Both women watch Uffe pick up the post that Alicia has arranged on the table and leave the house for his office, a converted milking parlor just across the yard.

It occurs to Alicia that the swing bridge doesn't go up now the sea has frozen over. There are no sailing boats using the canal between Sjoland and Mariehamn. Why did Uffe say it did?

Hilda wraps her arms around her body and turns toward Alicia.

'It was awful. We were this close from ending up in the freezing water!'

She lifts her hand up and indicates with her thumb and finger a minuscule distance. Alicia considers whether this is another case of exaggeration on her mother's part or whether something quite sinister has occurred.

'What happened then?'

'What do you mean?'

'To the man in the Jeep? Did he stop to see if you were alright?'

Hilda shakes her head. 'No, he just carried on. The thing is, he could have overtaken us easily without trying to ram us! There was no one coming from the other direction, and you know how slowly Uffe drives these days. With all this fresh snow, he was even more careful.'

Alicia nods. Uffe's overly cautious driving has become a concern to her almost as much as her mother's speeding. She wonders if he can't see that well anymore, because he seems to go everywhere at about 30 kilometers per hour. Luckily there isn't that much traffic on the islands, and there are many older drivers who are equally dawdling, and they don't mind.

It could just be that whoever was in the Jeep got frustrated following Uffe.

Still.

Alicia thinks for a moment. She's confused by Uffe's obvious lie about the swing bridge. Perhaps the two of them have had another of their rows and that's why he didn't try to calm Hilda down? Or refute her dramatic tale?

Suddenly her mother's mood changes.

'The house looks wonderful! And you've managed to clear the lane and the paths. That must have been hard? Fresh snow can be really heavy and you haven't done that in years!'

'Oh, Patrick helped out,' the words come out of Alicia's mouth before she has time to think.

'He did!' Hilda exclaims. Her eyebrows shoot up and she looks inquiringly at Alicia.

'As a favor to a friend. We were in the office yesterday afternoon when it started snowing and he offered, in case I needed help this morning.' Alicia is trying to keep her voice steady.

'Uh, uh,' Hilda says, giving Alicia a look that she knows far too well. The brief affair she had with her now work colleague—and boss, to be precise—is still a little raw, and her mother is one of the few people on the islands who suspects that they had a relationship.

'Nothing's going on,' she says, and trying to change the subject, adds, 'Did this Jeep scratch your car? And how did you know the driver was Russian?'

'He's a business associate of Uffe's.'

Alicia can hardly believe her ears.

'Really?'

'Yes, he's had some dealings with him, but that's all done now, so I'm not sure why he didn't even acknowledge us—or Uffe. And our car is fine. Uffe steered out of his way just in time.'

Alicia is staring at her mother.

'What are you telling me?'

Hilda bends down, unzips her boots, and pulls them off her feet. 'That's better,' she exclaims.

'These are so uncomfortable, but they look pretty, don't they? Very trendy someone told me in Spain.'

Her mother gives Alicia a coquettish look.

'There was this man who was so lovely. If I had my time again.' Hilda's eyes take on a dreamy quality. 'We had a fantastic time, sun and Sangria all the way!'

'That's nice,' Alicia replies, but her mind is racing. Why would her mother and stepfather have anything to do with a Russian driving a Cherokee? Those people were rumored to be part of the mafia, something Alicia has been quietly researching since she started working at the local newspaper, *Ålandsbladet*, last summer. She's seen some pretty awful accusations in local blogs and Facebook groups, but nothing that she could actually substantiate enough to write about. She hasn't even told Patrick, who's now the news editor, about her private investigations.

FOUR

Four days after she first stepped onboard MS *Sabrina* Brit is met at the apartment in Mariehamn by her old schoolfriend, Mia Eriksson. Wearing a pair of camel colored Sorel snow boots with a long, white Moncler padded coat, Mia looks for all the world like the heiress that she is. Her father, Kurt Eriksson, owns the local newspaper, *Ålandsbladet*, half the islands and much of Finland and Sweden too. Including the block of apartments in Mariehamn overlooking the sounds where the ferries pass on their way in and out of Mariehamn West Harbor, and where the two women are now standing.

Brit gazes at the magnificent view over the icy sea. 'Seeing the ships pass won't remind you too much of work, will it? On your days off, I mean?' Mia asks her.

Mia has thrown her coat on one of the pale gray sofas that face each other in the large living room.

Brit nearly laughs. This view commands a premium

price on the islands, and Mia thinks it'll bother her to look at it?

'That's so sweet of you to worry about me!' she exclaims instead. 'I am very grateful, you know. You must thank your Dad.'

Mia's expression hardens for a moment, then she comes and gives Brit one of her tight hugs. Her thin but strong arms envelop Brit. Pulling away, she adds, almost as an aside, 'I run the property side of the business now so I don't need to consult him.'

Brit realizes her mistake and says, quickly, 'Of course, sorry. You did say! I'm still a bit tired and jet-lagged.'

When she sees Mia's sideways smile from where she has gone to stand by the large windows again, Brit adds, 'You know, I've had so much going on, since being back.'

Mia's expression changes and, with more kindness in her voice, she says, 'You must be exhausted after your first shift. And here I am keeping you. Don't mind me, I'm off. Send me a message when you want to meet up. Lunch tomorrow, perhaps?'

With that Mia picks up her coat and is gone.

Brit sits down and looks around the luxurious place she will now call home. It's fully furnished with expensive-looking sofas and chairs. There's a kitchen separated from the living room by an island, topped with gray marble. All the equipment is new, as are the beds, linen, and fittings in the other two rooms, leading off from the small hall-way. The apartment is nine floors up, affording an amazing view of Ålands Hav.

Brit gets up and opens the fridge door. She puts her

hand over her mouth and gives out a short laugh. It seems her friend has stocked up with the essentials. Well, essentials as far as Mia is concerned. There's a bottle of Sancerre, one of Moët and two bottles of San Pellegrino water. A further investigation reveals a packet of sliced cheese, a carton of milk, a couple of tomatoes, a packet of gravlax and a quinoa salad inside a plastic container. There are six eggs in a box and tubs of both butter and olive spread. Brit goes into the larder and finds rye bread, sliced sourdough, Fazer chocolate, coffee capsules for the Nespresso machine standing on the counter, some fancy brown and white sugar sticks, and expensive looking ginger biscuits.

Brit grabs her phone and sends a thank you message with a heart emoji to Mia. She then opens the bottle of white and, finding a Riedel wine glass in a cupboard above the sink, pours herself a few mouthfuls and a sends a selfie to Mia too.

She sinks down on the sofa and wonders what the price of all this luxury will be. Is Mia simply in need of a friend? At school they didn't really mix, but after meeting up again a few months ago, they started to follow each other on Instagram and send the odd message back and forth. When Brit told Mia she was planning to come back to the islands, she offered her use of the apartment. Brit knows she's paying far below the going rate in rent, and now all these goodies just for her. She takes another sip from her glass and presses the bridge of her nose between her eyes.

She's tired.

Brit's first shift onboard wasn't a complete disaster. Apart from Kerstin, who seemed to take a dislike to her from the get go, most of the other restaurant staff are friendly and efficient. As is the Captain. Brit smiles at the memory of her first meeting with Jukka. She's sworn not to fall for a man ever again, but what's the harm in having a little flirtation? Jukka Markusson is handsome, about her age, and seemingly unattached. That much she was able to glean from that sour puss Kerstin. Brit enjoyed seeing the Captain's surprise when she looked straight into his eyes. Over the years she'd been engaged to an Italian Casanova, she had developed a few tricks of her own. Now all she had to do was wait for Jukka to come to her. Which he was certainly doing. During the first three sailings between the islands and Finland and Sweden, he had found a reason to call on Brit, or 'accidentally' bump into her, a total of ten times.

Brit has to admit that she's attracted to him. With his tall frame, wide smile and pale blue eyes, Jukka is nothing like Nico. He has none of the Italian's natural charm, but then it was time for a change! On the last leg, an early morning sailing from Stockholm, Brit had found an excuse to join Jukka on the bridge well before the start of her shift. She'd heard from the other staff that the Captain had a habit of being there well before anyone else had got out of their bunks.

Jukka was surprised but clearly delighted at her sudden appearance and willingly showed Brit the equipment, explaining with great patience the working of the satellite navigation, steering, and various cameras. Once, when they had been leaning over some control panel, heads close, their eyes met, and Brit had made out the darker rings inside Jukka's pale irises, as well as the perfectly formed light brown eyebrows and the specks of closely shaven hairs on his square jaw. His lips were slightly open, his breathing coming in shallow, short bursts. Just as Brit was thinking their proximity was lasting longer than was necessary, an alarm sounded somewhere and they'd both straightened themselves up.

'It's just the bow door checks,' Jukka said and gave a brief cough. Without looking at her, he began talking into an intercom, saying something Brit couldn't quite comprehend.

'I'll let you get on,' she said and smiled at Jukka, who turned to wave goodbye.

'Another time, I'll give you a more comprehensive tour of the controls, and even the engine room, if you wish.'

Brit nodded and widened her smile.'

'If it interests you, that is,' Jukka said uncertainly. 'Sorry, I get carried away with this stuff sometimes.'

Brit took a step toward him, and placed her hand on the Captain's arm, just above the epaulettes, the golden stripes stitched onto his uniform jacket.

Keeping her eyes steady on Jukka, she said, 'I'd like that very much.'

FIVE

On Monday, the skies are blue and the sun is low but surprisingly strong. It's blinding when the rays hit the snow boulders gathered on the sides of the road. The white fields that Alicia passes as she drives her old Volvo into town are glinting as if with a sprinkling of tiny diamonds. She has to lower the sun visor to shade her eyes.

Alicia had decided to stay overnight with Hilda and Uffe in the main house, rather than go back to the sauna cottage. During the two weeks they were away, she had slept in the house. With the snow and the low temperatures, it was more comfortable than her little cottage. Besides, she hadn't asked Patrick to shovel the snow from her own small driveway. It was awkward enough to have him in the main house. He hadn't been back to Alicia's sauna cottage since he left in a hurry when Liam surprised them in a most compromising situation last July. Alicia doesn't wish to relive that moment.

Uffe had got up early that morning, and by the time

Alicia was having her morning coffee, he had already cleared the path so Alicia could drive the Volvo down to the cottage and set the wood burner going for the day. By the evening she will be able to return to her own space.

The sauna cottage is really only meant for summer living, and Alicia knows she needs to make a decision about her future on the islands, something Liam keeps asking her about. She knows she wants to stay, she feels she belongs here, but what about Liam and their marriage?

As Alicia drives over the Sjoland canal bridge, she sees the slow-flowing, freezing water, and shrugs away thoughts of her mother and Uffe in that fatally icy water, trying to scramble out of their low sports car with their aging limbs. There's no way they would have survived that, she thinks and shivers. Then she thinks about her grief counsellor in London who had told her that she mustn't always picture the worst scenario. Alicia turns her mind toward her own complicated life instead. As if that would bring her more peace!

She thinks back to her whirlwind romance with her husband, which had started nearly twenty years ago, at Uppsala University. Alicia was studying English and Liam was a newly qualified doctor, attending a medical conference there. Since then, both Liam and Alicia had broken their marriage vows. Alicia always feels his infidelity was worse than hers. Liam's liaison with a nurse from the hospital where he has a private clinic had been carrying on for months, while Alicia and Patrick's affair was just a matter of weeks.

A few crazy weeks.

There's no way Liam will want to leave his clinic in London. That's not the 'changes' he was talking about, Alicia is sure of that. He loves his job as a surgeon, and will under no circumstances want to leave London. Would they be able to carry on a relationship while living so far apart? Sometimes Alicia thinks that the physical distance is the least difficult part of their current marital problems. It's far harder to overcome the sudden loss of their son, or what happened after Stefan's death, or rather what Liam had been up to with his nurse. And then last summer, Alicia herself was unfaithful with Patrick. Their relationship is now totally professional and platonic. They have both moved on, so Patrick isn't causing a problem in her marriage. Not as far as Alicia is concerned, anyhow.

The image of Patrick standing in the doorway, looking tall, rugged and so blond, enters Alicia's mind, but she shrugs off the attraction she still feels toward him. She's sure it's natural. After such an explosive affair, her body is bound to react to his closeness.

The elation of the birth of their granddaughter, something neither Alicia or Liam had imagined could happen after losing their son at the tender age of seventeen, had wiped out the importance of their infidelities.

But slowly, over the fall months, Alicia's belief in a future with her husband has started to wane. It isn't that she wants to get back with Patrick. She can't imagine they will ever be good for each other. Patrick's marriage is over, but he still has two daughters who need him and an ex who is more than demanding. Not to mention her family, the wealthy Erikssons. It's far too complicated, and her feelings for the man have changed, she's sure of that. They are just friends and work colleagues now. Alicia shrugs off thoughts of how handsome Patrick looked on Sunday morning. She has a new life now, with a new granddaughter and she doesn't need men.

The road veers toward the left and climbs a small hill. In the distance, on her left, she spots the low buildings of Mariehamn, the capital city of the Åland islands, its lights reflected in the white landscape. The rising sun is low behind Hotel Arkipelag and its wide 70's style windows look dark and empty.

The West Harbor in front of the hotel is now void of sailing boats and there's a thick layer of snow on the jetties that jut out into the ice-covered water. She shrugs away her summer memories of spending a day on Patrick's yacht. She can still picture his body. Sometimes, the desire to touch him is overwhelming when he's standing close to her. But she's managed to keep a distance and remain true to her promise to try to settle things with Liam. Working together with a former lover isn't ideal, but they have managed to forge some kind of professional relationship since the summer and the birth of her and Liam's granddaughter.

Thoughts of little Anne Sofie bring a smile to Alicia's lips. Set against her love for the child, the problems she has with the men in her life pale into insignificance, though Anne Sofie is one of the reasons she's trying to work things out with Liam. Poor Frida, now completely on her own after her mother passed away last month, needs help and that is what Alicia intends to provide—a support network to catch the gorgeous baby and her mother if they fall. Wouldn't any grandmother, but especially one whose only son is dead, do the same?

This Christmas—the baby's first—will be one where the family will truly come together. Hilda has already planned a feast for them all on Christmas Eve, when the main celebration takes place. Liam is arriving two days before this, and Alicia has a list of foodstuffs to be bought and prepared, as well as a few last-minute gifts she needs to get in Mariehamn in the coming days. She's lucky that her job at *Ålandsbladet* is far from demanding. She can nip out during her long lunch hour, and leave early whenever she wishes. In theory, she's still a part-timer, but she finds it better to keep to a Monday to Friday routine, only taking the occasional day off. And it has nothing to do with being with Patrick every day, which was something Liam had suggested when she mentioned his name in passing during a video call. Alicia was annoyed with Liam at first, then found it funny. Sticking to a routine had nothing to do with Patrick. But when she saw Liam's expression, she wondered if there could be some truth in it. No, there really wasn't. Patrick and Alicia are work colleagues, and perhaps could be called friends. That's all.

SIX

When Alicia enters the newspaper office she glances around the open space. There are three other reporters there, their eyes trained on their screens, though they lift them momentarily to nod a hello to her. Patrick, who now officially works at the paper as the news editor, hasn't yet arrived. She is relieved. He sits opposite her, behind a screen. If she lifts her head, she can see the top of his blond head and his bright blue eyes. She's thought about moving desks, but that in itself would show that it bothers her to sit so close to him every day. Which it doesn't, usually.

But on Sunday she had felt that Patrick was about to say something personal to her. She shouldn't have accepted his offer to clear the snow. He's featured far too heavily in her thoughts during the drive into Mariehamn, too, something she wouldn't have been able to hide from him if he had been there. Relief, mixed with a sense of disappointment, washes over her.

Alicia opens her email program and tries to banish

thoughts of Patrick. Scrolling down her emails, she sees that there has been an accident on one of the ferry-boats connecting the other islands to Mariehamn. That in itself is unusual and she's relieved she'll have something a little more engaging to write about that morning. But when she reads on, her interest is further piqued.

A black Jeep Cherokee collided with another car as it disembarked at Föglö.

There was no driver's name or any other details.

Alicia taps a number on her phone.

'Ebba, Alicia here. Do you have time to talk?'

'Yes,' The police chief says in her habitual curt way.

'The collision in Föglö. Can you tell me anything about it?'

There is a silence at the other end of the telephone. Alicia waits. She is now used to her old schoolfriend's manner, and she knows that if she tries to rush Ebba, she'll get even less information from her.

'What do you want to know? And why?'

Alicia tries to keep her voice level as she replies, 'Name, address, that sort of thing. It's a slow news day so anything is welcome. Give me all the information you have. Or *can* give me.'

Alicia just remembers to add the last sentence. She knows how seriously her friend takes her duties as the new police chief on the islands.

Ebba gives Alicia the names of the drivers, and Alicia gasps when she hears the name of the Cherokee driver. A Russian!

'The driver of the Mazda doesn't want to press

charges, but we'll still investigate. On behalf of the state, since the incident occurred on a public highway.'

With these words in her official, dry voice, Ebba ends the call.

After she's put down the phone Alicia gets to work on finding a photograph of Sergei Dudnikov, the Cherokee driver. She is certain this is the same man who caused such commotion between Uffe and Hilda that morning. The timings work perfectly. If the man in the car that had tried to ram into her mother and stepfather's car had driven at speed through Sjoland to the ferryboat that runs between the smaller islands, he would just have made the 3.40 sailing, which arrives on the island of Föglö at 4.10 pm. Besides, these kinds of cars aren't very common in Åland. What are the chances that two black Jeeps of exactly the same model would be traveling over the Sjoland swing bridge? Ebba had said that it had been quite a smash, with damage to the bumper, a broken headlight, and scratches to the driver's door of the other vehicle—a small Mazda. The image of the large American SUV ramming a small Japanese passenger car to smithereens makes Alicia shiver.

She peers toward the glazed office at the end of the open-plan space and sees it's unoccupied. The black leather chair of the editor, a man of few words, Harri Noutiainen, is empty inside the glass cubicle. She goes over to a new intern called Kim.

'I'm off, following up on a story.'

Kim, who has strawberry blonde hair that sticks out in all directions and a long face, matching his lanky frame, nods. Alicia smiles as she turns to leave the office.

She hasn't got more than a handful of words out of Kim since he started in September. The boy is painfully shy. A deep blush covers his freckles if Alicia tries to engage him in any kind of conversation, so she mostly lets him be. He does his job well, and has a very precise writing style. As long as he overcomes his shyness, he'll make a great reporter.

SEVEN

After a morning spent hauling the boxes containing her possessions from the underground parking lot up to her apartment, Brit drives her Golf east out of Mariehamn. In the night she'd woken with alarm, not knowing where she was, but when she saw the white headboard of the bed, she remembered she was in Mia Eriksson's luxurious apartment. In the small hours, she realized this was her first night back in Åland for over six months.

Too long to be away from home.

She now needs to catch a ferry to Föglö, but by the time she's driving over the Sjoland bridge, something that was a slight snowfall when she left Mariehamn is turning into a full-blown snowstorm.

Tiny white flecks are swirling in front of her, nearly obscuring the road ahead. Briefly, she considers turning back, but decides that she'll make her way slowly to the small ferry port, which is some twenty minutes away. If the ferry is cancelled due to the bad weather, she will turn around and telephone her father from the apartment. She feels she needs to see him as soon as possible—it's been too long since her last visit.

To Brit's surprise when she arrives at the port, there's another car waiting on the tarmac. In the distance, she can just make out that something is approaching the small jetty. Through the blizzard, the shape of the car ferry slowly becomes more recognizable, and suddenly it's in front of her. After a single car gets out of the belly of the boat, Brit and the driver of the other car are able to drive onboard.

Brit's father lives in an old wooden house on the outer edges of the small island of Föglö. He will tell anyone who wants to hear that he built the wooden red house with a steel roof himself in the early sixties, before Brit was born. After her mother had succumbed to cancer when Brit was still a teenager, many of her father's friends advised him to move to an apartment in Mariehamn to make it easier for Brit to attend school and for him to cope without his beloved Angelica. But Rolf had built the house when he was a young man, newly in love with the prettiest girl he'd ever set eyes on, so he stayed.

As Brit approaches the house along the long drive lined with high banks of snow, cleared by Rolf's old tractor, Brit wonders if it might be time to broach the subject of a move to Mariehamn again, now he is in his mid-seventies. She has traveled the world, never staying in one place for too long, and cannot imagine a whole life lived in the same small community on an island, often cut off from Fasta Aland, the main island. She remembers many a day when she couldn't make it to school because the ferries were cancelled on account of stormy weather.

When Rolf Svensson opens the door, Brit is taken aback by how old and thin he looks.

'Are you eating regularly?' Brit asks when they are sitting at the kitchen table, drinking coffee out of old faded china cups, part of her parents' wedding gifts, that were used only for "best."

Her father laughs.

'I'm fine, don't you worry about me.'

Looking at his wrinkled face, with his sad droopy eyes, visibly filled with cataracts, Brit places her manicured hand over her father's bony thin one.

'Still no man then?' Rolf says, lifting his eyes, which wrinkle at the corners as he smiles.

This is their game. Every time Brit comes back to the islands, he asks about a boyfriend.

'Nearly got there with a Rat of an Italian,' Brit says, surprising herself. She feels a lump in her throat and looks away from her father's direct gaze.

Rolf pulls his hand from underneath hers and pats it. 'You're beautiful and clever, any man would be a fool not to see that.'

'Oh, *Pappa*, I've missed you!' Brit says, tears pricking her eyes. She gets up and hugs her dad, noting how thin and fragile his frame is. Again, she wonders if she should mention a move to some kind of sheltered accommodation in town. Now that she is in Mariehamn, she would be able to visit him even more frequently if he was close by.

Sitting back down and accepting another cup of coffee, Brit decides to leave the matter until her next visit.

'So you are living in one of Eriksson's apartments?'

'Yes. Do you remember Mia was a class below me in the Lyceum?'

Rolf nods and pours some cream into his coffee.

'Well, she came on one of the cruises with her husband and we sort of became friends. So she helped me get the apartment.

Rolf lifts one busy eyebrow. 'I hear they've divorced?'

Now it's Brit's turn to lift her lips into a smile. 'Not much gets past you.'

'It was in the *World Sheet.*'

'Really? Mia didn't tell me that,' Brit says. Then she laughs, 'You still call *Ålandsbladet* that?'

There's a glint in her father's eyes, and his smile widens briefly. Then he says, 'You managing the rent? I hear they are worth a lot of money those new monstrosities.'

Brit crosses her arms. Typical of her father to think anything new is a monstrosity. Again Brit pats her father's hand. 'I'm all grown-up now, *Pappa.*'

Brit says goodbye to her father, who in spite of her protests, stands outside in the chill wind to wave her off as she walks along the path to her car. Even though she is alarmed to think how a strong gust could whisk Rolf off, a sense of great peace descends on her as she leaves the house where she was born. She knows she should have visited Åland and her father more often, but now—at last—

she is here permanently. She'll be able to see him once a week, if not more often. Although he looked frail, Brit could see he had chopped wood for the burner in the lounge. The logs were stacked outside the house, covered with tarpaulin and a thick layer of snow, a small corner showing where her father had picked up a few logs each day. She knows that his neighbors, a Finnish couple who moved into the house about twenty years ago, help Rolf with tasks and looked in on him when there was bad weather, or if he hadn't been seen for a day or so. Perhaps they helped her father chop the logs?

They were a nice couple but Brit always had the sense that they didn't approve of her lifestyle, which kept her away from her father for months at a time.

Brit sighs with satisfaction when she looks in her rear-view mirror and sees her father go inside and close the door. From now on she would be here to help and Rolf's neighbors would have nothing to reproach her for.

EIGHT

Patrick sits in the kitchen of his apartment on the tenth floor of a new development overlooking the frozen sea. That morning's cruise ferries have just passed by his window, making their way toward the shipping lanes, cutting the ice beyond the East Harbor in half. There's a sharp wind, with snow flurries swirling up and down and settling on the bannister of his balcony outside. The skies are dark and there's a threat of a full-blown snow storm in the air.

He has just put the phone down to his former boss, the editor of *Journalen* in Stockholm. He smiles to himself, pleased with the decision he's made. Now all he needs to do is convince Alicia to come with him. Once again, he gazes out of the vast floor-to-ceiling windows, which wrap around the kitchen and living area of the apartment. He will not even miss this view. He will not regret leaving Mariehamn behind, or the rows with Mia, or the Eriksson family, whose influence is everywhere on the islands. He fought hard to get his two daughters, Sara and Alexandra, for two weekends a month, and he knows they will be delighted to spend those in Stockholm. Already nearly teenagers, they will revel in being in a capital city rather than in this small provincial island town.

He'd much rather be sitting overlooking Kungsholmen over the water from the buzzy Södermalm part of Stockholm. How he misses the trendy restaurants and cafés, which serve his morning lattes just perfectly. Where *not everyone* knows who he is, and watches his every move.

Patrick has spent his summers in this quirky island community ever since he married Mia over ten years ago, and he has grown to love Åland in his way. But he'd never spent a long fall and winter on the islands until now. And he's never worked on a small newspaper like the *Ålandsbladet* before, where a theft of a flower pot is considered a newsworthy item. He misses the hustling he had to do while working at the *Journalen*. He isn't ashamed to admit that he enjoys the thrill of chasing a real news story, whether it's a senseless knifing of a teenager, or a calculated murder of a loved (or previously loved) partner. He also enjoyed the interaction with the hardened Stockholm police officers, who didn't want to give him any information unless it was in their interest to let the criminals know what they knew. And he has to admit it to himself, winning a prize for his journalism had always been a dream. It wasn't too late, he was only thirty-seven, a full eight years younger than the previous year's winner of Sweden's Journalist of the Year.

That's never going to happen if you stay here in this tiny group of islands in the middle of the Baltic Sea!

Patrick's thoughts return to Alicia. Again, if he is

truthful, the reason he has stayed in Åland is to a large extent because of her presence. Of course, being close to his daughters has been a large motivation to stay too, but the journey to Stockholm is so short, four hours on the ferry, and Sara and Alexandra can hop over the Ålands Hav any time they want.

What Patrick needs to do is to convince Alicia to come with him to Stockholm. Since their brief affair last summer, he hasn't stopped thinking about her. And he knows that she and Liam are hardly getting on. He's only been to see her a couple of times since the summer, and Patrick can tell from Alicia's face and her body language that they're not sleeping together. At least he thinks they're not. The thought makes his heart beat fast and he notices that he's formed fists with his hands, so he decides not to think about it.

He's just not got over her. Which has really surprised him. He's tried seeing other women in Stockholm, not here in the gossip-ridden small circles of Mariehamn, but to no avail. However blonde, leggy, and pretty, they just haven't interested him enough to warrant a second date.

When Alicia sent him a message yesterday, accepting his offer of help with the snow at the Ulsson's place, he was certain she wanted something else too. But when he hinted at wanting to talk about more than the mundane, she had clammed up.

He's got to get her on his own soon and talk to her properly.

NINE

Alicia drives her old Volvo back over the swing bridge into Sjoland. She passes Hilda and Uffe's house and her own temporary home, the sauna cottage, as she makes her way toward the small ferry port at the end of the island. It's now snowing heavily, the sunshine of the morning but a memory. Momentarily Alicia's mind drifts to the forthcoming Christmas celebrations. A thick covering of snow over the landscape is perfect for her plans to create a wonderful *Jul*.

Alicia turns her thoughts to her destination. She's taken this car ferry many times to the outer islands whether on an excursion with school, or when invited to the birthday parties of friends who lived in the outer archipelago. Föglö is one of the larger outcrops, which has a permanent population. It's part of the complicated ferry traffic that criss-cross the Åland islands. From memory, she pictures a restaurant overlooking the water, which is a popular venue for summer parties. But in the winter the ferry is mainly used by locals, which makes

Alicia wonder if the Russian has a place somewhere in Föglö or farther on. Perhaps he lives here permanently? She ponders the various possibilities as she arrives in the port and sees the ferry making its slow progress toward her.

The falling snow is now dense and the wind has got up. Alicia can just make out the water in the shipping lane, which is the color of steel and moves slowly, like thick oil, at the bow of the ship. Alicia pulls her coat closer when she sees from her phone that the temperature has plummeted. She's glad of her long, warm padded parka, which Hilda had given her from the leftover stock of her shop.

Briefly, Alicia wonders how much money her mother and Uffe lost when they decided to close the fashion boutique. The space is now taken up by a men's hair-dressers. When Alicia saw the new sign, 'Gentlemen's Barber Shop' written in an old-fashioned curvaceous font, she thought no one in Åland would pay through the nose for a shave or a haircut. It had seemed far too trendy for the islands. But the shop is still there, and even in winter there's always someone in a red leather chair, having their faces lathered with foam. She has heard rumors that the enterprise is being financed by Russian mafia, but as usual, when it comes to this kind of talk on the islands, her research into the money side has borne no fruit.

Alicia's is the only car waiting to board, and when the bow of the ship opens, she sees just two vehicles emerge and drive past her toward Mariehamn. Once onboard,

Alicia makes her way to the upper deck where the passengers sit. There are three other people already there, one couple and a lone female foot passenger, looking out to sea. The snow and chill wind nearly convince Alicia to turn back when, moments later, she climbs the outer stairs from the forehead deck to the bridge. She wants to talk to the staff onboard.

'Didn't see it,' the First Mate says. He's standing half in, half out of the bridge, while holding the door to the gangway open with one foot. He's smoking a roll-up cigarette and he smells of diesel oil and the sea.

'But who reported the accident to the police?' Alicia asks. She's also trying to engage the Captain in the discussion, but he glances only briefly in her direction. He's by the control panel, his eyes trained on the horizon, where the teal-blue sea of the shipping lane meets the now dim, white sky. The visibility is poor and Alicia wonders if the ferry is on autopilot. It's past 2pm and it will be dusk in an hour or so. The Captain, who wears a worn-looking jacket with dirty gold braid on the sleeves, has sandy colored hair and dark eyes, the exact shade of the sea in the shipping lane. Both men are tall and look weather-beaten, with unshaven chins and calloused hands: archetypical sailors.

The First Mate shrugs and flicks his cigarette out over the rail and into the water. Alicia wonders about the safety of smoking onboard. Surely it must be illegal, but she says nothing.

'Close that damn door,' the Captain bellows suddenly, and the First Mate nods to Alicia. He lifts his foot away and the coils on the door spring into action, closing it quickly.

'Wait,' Alicia says and takes hold of the door handle and slips inside the bridge. It's a large space, almost entirely taken up by the control panel at the front. Alicia's coat and hair are wet, she feels like a drowned cat.

She hears the Captain take a deep breath. 'We didn't see anything,' he now says, turning his head fully toward Alicia.

'Take over, will you?' he says to the First Mate and comes to stand close to her. 'It happened before we docked. So there's nothing we can tell you.'

'But,' Alicia begins, but the Captain opens the door behind her and a gust of wind lifts Alicia's hair up, blowing snow and strands of wet hair into her face. She tries to wipe her face and scrape the hair behind her ear. 'The police chief told me the Jeep Cherokee drove into the Mazda when it was boarding the ship,' she says, holding onto her hair, trying to control it.

'Look, lady, we're at sea, and no one is allowed on the bridge while the ferry in in transit. I told you we didn't see the accident and that's that. You're not police, so bugger off.'

When the ferry arrives at Föglö, Alicia can see both men looking at her through the wide glass on the high bridge.

If I've ever seen anyone lie badly, those two did today.

TEN

Ebba has sent her the full details of the other person involved in the rear-ender. He's the manager of the K-Market. Alicia is relieved to see that it's a convenience store right in the center of Föglö. Lars Mortenson turns out of be a youngish man with a large belly hanging over his jeans, and an untidy wispy beard covering his double chin. His mousy hair is short, and he wears small glasses, making his head seem large and round. He walks slowly toward Alicia along the central aisle of the grocery store. Alicia stands by the tills, eyed suspiciously by the young girl with pink hair, who called Lars over the tannoy.

'Who are you?' Lars Mortenson says in response to Alicia's question about the accident.

'Alicia O'Connell from *Ålandsbladet*,' she replies with a smile, but Lars doesn't take her outstretched hand.

He turns away. 'Nothing to tell you. An accident, pure and simple.'

'Not what the police tell me,' Alicia says, following the

man along the shop floor to the back where the chilled goods are. The man turns left and opens a door marked *Private*.

'I have nothing to say to you!' Lars Mortenson bangs the door in Alicia's face.

While she's been in the store, the snow has been falling heavily and there's a thick blanket on her car. She can hardly distinguish the land from the sea, or make out the port, even though she knows it's less than a kilometer along the shore.

Visibility on the road is dreadful as Alicia turns carefully out of the parking lot. At the junction to the main road of the island, she's grateful that all of Föglö has decided to stay at home. She prays the ferry traffic isn't affected by the sudden turn in the weather. The last thing she needs is to get stuck on the other side of water. She tries to think if she knows anyone on the island, but only comes up with the father of a friend who works abroad. She doesn't know how old he is, or if he's even still alive. Besides, he may not even remember Alicia.

The summer restaurant has a few rooms to rent, but that will be shut now. She tries to stop herself from panicking and tells herself that the ferries operate in all sorts of weather conditions. There's still 30 minutes until the sailing, and she's glad to spot the outline of a red hut, used as a waiting room, next to the small port.

At that very moment, a car drives toward her at speed. All she has time to register is a large black lump, surrounded by clouds of white.

ELEVEN

Everything is a blur. Alicia turns the steering wheel and ends up hitting one of the snowy boulders on the side of the road. She hears the roar of an engine as the vehicle passes her and then silence. She glances in her rear-view mirror. Through the falling snow she sees the clear outline of a Jeep Cherokee, its engine running empty in the middle of the road. After a moment, it begins to reverse.

'Do you need help?' a man about Alicia's age, with large pale eyes, is gazing down at her through the driver's window of the elevated SUV. He's speaking English with a soft Russian accent.

'You tried to hit me,' Alicia blurts out. This must be the same man who tried to run her mother and Uffe off the road and who'd driven into the manager of the K-Market.

For a moment, a small smile plays on the lips of the man in the car, but it's so fleeting that Alicia later wonders if she'd imagined it.

'I lost control of the steering for a while. I'm so sorry. May I help you out of the ditch? I have some ropes in the car.'

There is absolutely no one about and the ferry that is supposed to take her back home to Sjoland is still nowhere to be seen. Alicia nods and the man gets out of the car.

'You're Alicia, Uffe's daughter, aren't you?' he says after he's managed to pull Alicia's old Volvo back onto the road. The man is now standing next to her car, with the snow falling onto his thin, fair hair. His ears are red from the cold, but he doesn't make any effort to pull up the collar of his thick, expensive-looking down coat. Instead, he takes off a leather glove and offers Alicia his hand.

'Alexander Dudnikov,' he says.

For a moment Alicia considers ignoring the man and just driving off, but her journalistic training kicks in and she takes Dudnikov's hand. His grip around her fingers is strong and warm.

'You can call me Alex,' he says. The lines around his eyes deepen as his mouth lifts into a smile.

'So what happened back there? Why did you drive into me? Can't be the same reason you nearly destroyed Lars Mortenson's Mazda yesterday?'

The Russian stands in front of Alicia. The snow is falling, with gusts of wind occasionally making the landscape around them disappear into a soft, white haze.

'Yes, of course, you work for Kurt's paper, don't you?' Dudnikov says after a long while. Although there are no threatening words in his question, there's something sinister in his voice.

'And you know everybody,' Alicia says, her eyes steady on the man standing by the side of her car. She has to look up at him, giving her a disadvantage, but she's trying to ignore the obvious power he has over her. There's no one around, and the visibility is so bad, with white flurries dancing around them, that even if there was someone inside the red hut at the side of the port, waiting for the ferry, through the small windows they wouldn't be able to discern more than the shape of the two cars and perhaps those of Alicia and the Russian standing by the side of the road.

Dudnikov smiles at Alicia, but doesn't speak, so Alicia adds, 'You may be interested to know that I have already talked to Lars Mortenson. Perhaps you'd like to make a statement now.'

'I'm a very bad driver, I'm afraid,' Dudnikov says, with a widening smile. His gaze stays on Alicia when he adds, 'I believe your ferry will soon be here. If I were you, I'd forget about stories of silly little bumps and return home. You don't want to get stuck on this island all on your own. Have a good day.'

Dudnikov turns to open the door to his Jeep. Inside, he winds down his window. 'I'm sure we'll meet again soon.'

Once inside the car, Alicia shivers in her seat. She starts the engine of the Volvo, which purrs with a comforting sound. Before she moves, she looks through the open window and sees the shape of the black Jeep fade as it moves away from her.

TWELVE

While she's been with her father, the storm has abated a little. Still, it's difficult to see the road ahead through the intermittent flurries of drifting snow, so Brit takes it easy on her way toward the small Föglö ferry port. On a good day she can make it from her father's house in less than ten minutes, but today she's left much more time for the short drive.

At the port, Brit is suddenly aware of a black shape in the middle of the road. She sees a large black American SUV—a rare sight in Mariehamn, let alone on the smaller islands—swerve in front of her, forcing her to break hard. Just before the two cars collide, the SUV corrects its course and drives past Brit. Blowing air out of her cheeks, Brit pulls onto the side of the road and checks her mirror. As the vehicle disappears from view, she sees that the car is a Cherokee, but she can't make out the number plates, only that a largish man is driving without a backward glance to see if she's OK.

Another bastard in a hurry, she thinks and puts her Golf

into gear. Only a few meters farther on she sees a Volvo on the side of the road, with a woman inside. She turns, and Brit cannot believe her eyes. Quickly, she parks behind the car and gets out.

'Alicia!'

'Brit!'

'What are you doing here?' Alicia says. She thinks her eyes are failing her, but here, on the road in Föglö, exposed to the dreadful weather stands her best and oldest schoolfriend. She climbs out of the car and stretches her arms out to give Brit a hug.

'I could ask you the same thing!' Brit says and takes hold of Alicia's shoulders. Brit is a little taller than Alicia. She suddenly remembers how she'd begged her mom for a pair of high-heeled boots just so that she'd be the same height as her friend. But Hilda hadn't budged. 'You'll fall and break your neck. And how would Madam get to classes then, eh?'

'That's a long story,' Alicia says, but her words are swallowed by a sudden snow flurry. The wind is whipping at their bodies, threatening to blow the two women away, so they decide to sit in the car.

'This weather! I've missed the snow but this!' Brit says sitting next to Alicia. She brushes flakes off her shoulders. She's wearing a brand-new padded coat over tight black jeans and fashionable looking snow-boots.

Alicia starts to laugh and soon they are both giggling, and they hug again awkwardly over the gearshift. Alicia sees that there are still snowflakes on top of Brit's dark hair and she wipes them off with her hand.

'I didn't know you're here? You've been to see your dad, I presume? I was just thinking about you and him.'

Brit nods. She tells Alicia about her new job at Marie Line and the apartment in Mariehamn. When she mentions the block and where it is, Alicia's heart stops for a moment.

'That's owned by the Eriksson family,' she says.

Brit nods, but before Alicia has time to ask any more about her friend's new home, Brit takes Alicia's hands into hers and says, 'I heard about Stefan. I'm so sorry.'

Alicia lifts her eyes toward her friend and nods. She's used to hearing condolences from people she knew when she was young on the islands, but to hear it from this particular friend takes the wind out of her lungs. When Alicia doesn't reply, Brit adds, 'Look, I know I should have come over to London, called you, or something, but I couldn't get away.' Brit bites her lip and adds, 'You know me. I'm a coward.'

'Oh, don't say that!' Alicia looks at her friend and squeezes the hands holding hers.

'I've only just surfaced from, you know. I wasn't myself for a long time. If that makes any sense.'

Brit nods. Alicia feels tears welling up inside her, so she changes the subject.

'Did you see that maniac? He nearly ran me off the road. All because,' Suddenly Alicia thinks it best not to divulge what she knows about the Russian until she's found out more and discussed her thoughts with the editor at *Ålandsbladet*.

'He did what?'

'Oh, just driving recklessly. You nearly came a cropper in the Golf, didn't you?'

Brit gazes at her friend, 'Hmm, I did.'

'But let's forget about that bastard. Are you here on holiday, or what?'

It takes so long for Alicia to tell her friend about what has happened to her in the past six months that halfway through, they spot the car ferry making its way toward the little port. They decide to drive on and carry on talking over a coffee onboard.

THIRTEEN

'Mia is nice now, honestly she's not at all as nasty as she used to be at school,' Brit says. Her manicured hands are hugging a white mug of hot, steaming coffee.

'Really?' Alicia says and adds, 'She doesn't much like me.'

'Why not?'

The boat rocks from side to side, and Alicia looks out of the window. The snow storm has rendered the view almost completely white. You cannot even make out the small outcrops that are scattered along this little crossing between Föglö and Sjoland.

Alicia turns her face back to her friend. 'How come you kept in touch with Mia Eriksson after school?' she asks. She feels a small prick of jealousy that Brit hasn't contacted her more than once or twice in all the years she was living in London. She's just reconnected with her best friend who is living back on the islands at exactly the same time as she is, and she's best friends with the person who probably considers Alicia to be Public Enemy Number One on Åland. Brit must have seen it in her face, or heard it in the tone of her voice, because she stretches her hand out and touches Alicia. 'Don't be like that. We'll never be best of pals, not really.' She glances at Alicia and adds, 'At least not like you and me.'

'I didn't mean that. God, we're not at school anymore!' Alicia says, and they both laugh, knowing that there really is no difference. To Alicia, seeing her friend feels as if she's been transported back to the small Mariehamn classroom, where boys threw paper planes at the girls they liked, and girls whispered amongst themselves about the boys they fancied. And the girls they disliked. Mia was always popular—she was thin and had the latest Spice Girls T-shirts and pencil cases.

It transpires that Mia and Patrick and the girls had been on a cruise boat that Brit worked on. 'It was amazing to see someone from the islands out there—hundreds of miles away.'

Brit tells Alicia that it was Mia who sought Brit's company each evening after her shift ended because Patrick wanted to go to bed early.

They must have already been fighting then, Alicia thinks.

'The guy is a complete loser,' Brit says.

'Oh?'

'Yeah, have you met him? Patrick?'

'Actually, I have. I work with him at *Ålandsbladet*.'

'My God, yes. He's an editor there now, isn't he? Mia told me it was part of the divorce settlement, to give him something to do.' Brit laughs and Alicia hears Mia's words coming out of her friend's mouth.

Brit studies her friend. Aware of this, Alicia tries to keep her face expressionless.

'Oh my God, you like him?'

'Patrick is a friend and colleague, that's all.'

'Oh, yeah?'

Alicia sees in her friend's green eyes that she knows Alicia is lying. It's strange that even though she hasn't seen Brit for over twenty years, it's as if they have spoken to each other every day since leaving school. Nothing has changed, apart from a few wrinkles around their eyes. Well, possibly Alicia's schoolfriend has gained a pound or two, but that's made her womanly shape even more attractive.

Alicia remembers that Brit had been the first one of all the girls in their year to have proper breasts. Suddenly, on the first day back from the summer holiday, when they were getting undressed before sports, she'd noticed Brit had an extra garment under her shirt. She remembers how nobody had commented on Brit's new bra, which was white with tiny pink roses, but how they had looked on in awe as she expertly unhooked it and revealed perfectly round mounds with pink nipples standing proud in the middle. They had all looked quickly away, but Alicia had seen from the corner of her eye that Brit had straightened her back ever so slightly. Then she had pulled out a white crop top from her sports bag. This, she later told Alicia, was her sports bra.

Brit was the more outgoing of the two friends, and was always dreaming of travel to exotic places. Her father was a sea captain—now retired, Alicia knew from her mother. It hadn't been a surprise to anyone when Brit had begun a career onboard luxury cruise ships rather than going to university in Sweden, like Alicia.

'So, spill the beans!' Brit now says, hers eyes wide, with a meaningful, demanding look.

Alicia tells Brit the whole sorry saga of her and Liam's break-up after she'd discovered his affair with a nurse at the hospital where he worked as a surgeon.

'It started after we lost Stefan.'

Alicia bites her lip. She feels the threat of tears, but takes a deep breath and continues. 'We'd been drifting apart for years without me noticing. When we came here for our usual holiday, things just got worse, so he went back home early and I decided to stay.'

'You decided to move back here from London–just like that?' Brit asks, her eyes even wider now.

'Look who's speaking!'

To this Brit gives one of her loud, cackling laughs that she was famous for at school. The teachers used to say they could hear her across the water between Föglö and Mariehamn.

'Fair point,' Brit says through giggles.

'You know what my mother is like,' Alicia begins and Brit, now quiet again, nods. Hilda wasn't like all the other mothers at school. She had great plans for Alicia's future and always demanded top marks at every exam she ever took. The other Åland parents were happy if their kids just passed each year without too many black marks on their record, but for Hilda nothing but top of the class was good enough.

'When I decided to stay on, she began talking about

getting me a job with the newspapers, so I decided to get one myself before she had time to interfere.'

'You met Patrick at *Ålandsbladet*?'

Alicia is quiet for a moment. She's not sure how much of their relationship she should reveal to her old friend who, by all accounts, is now best friends with Mia, Patrick's ex.

'I met Mia and Patrick on the ferry on our way here. That was just before they split up.'

'And?' Brit says, 'I can tell there's more!'

'We had a very brief fling.' As soon as the words come out of Alicia's mouth she regrets them. Being caught in the snow storm and the accident with the Russian must have messed with her head.

'What?' Brit's eyes are wide and her mouth stays open.

'If I tell you everything, you must promise not to say anything to anyone—especially Mia!'

'Who do you take me for!' Brit exclaims.

'OK, so you know I was under the impression that Liam and I had split up, and Mia had told Patrick about the other guy, so basically we were both free agents. It didn't work out that way, but at the time, I thought it might.'

Alicia looks at her friend. She doesn't know how Brit will react to an affair between two married people. When they last saw each other, Alicia had just met Liam and was madly in love. Brit was about to start her first job with a British cruise liner and they talked about meeting up in London, but the plan never materialized. Alicia was already pregnant–without knowing it–and about to head into the whirlwind that motherhood brings.

'Go on, I want all the details!' Brit now says, smiling. 'I can then tell you about The Rat of an Italian that I thought was the love of my life. And the new guy I met recently.'

'What? You've met someone? Where? When?' Alicia is desperate to change the subject. Normally Brit would be delighted to talk about herself, but this time, Alicia isn't so lucky.

'You first.' Brit says determinedly with a wicked grin on her face.

Alicia gives in and tells her friend how Patrick and Mia had invited her and Uffe and Hilda to the prestigious Eriksson Midsummer Party and how, by chance, the two of them had ended up on a beach that Patrick used to escape from his influential in-laws (and Mia). How he'd been swimming naked, how Alicia had had too much champagne, and how they'd ended up kissing.

When, a few days later, Patrick had asked Alicia to go sailing on his boat, she had succumbed to him. And then she had found out that her beloved son had got a local girl pregnant. She'd been so delighted by this news that she had even envisaged a future on the islands with Patrick, and the new granddaughter.

'Suddenly everything fell into place,' Alicia says.

Brit is quiet for a moment, then asks, 'Do you love him?'

Alicia hasn't really allowed herself to think whether she fell in love with Patrick last summer or not. Or how she really feels about him now. After Liam's protestations of love and his desire to try again, and the birth of little Anne Sofie, she hadn't even considered a future with Patrick. She wanted to keep her family together, and this now consisted of Liam, Frida, Ann Sofie and, of course, her parents. The only problem is Liam, who was still in London with no plans to move to the islands. And their relationship, which is another complication in itself.

Besides, Patrick's life was complicated too. With the divorce, and his fights with Mia over access to his daughters, it was easier to keep their relationship on a purely professional level. Alicia thinks back to the Sunday morning at Hilda and Uffe's house, when Patrick had wanted to talk to Alicia about something personal. But she must resist any return to last summer's craziness. She must keep her family together for the sake of her grand-daughter.

'No, I don't think so,' Alicia says, and for the first time since the previous July, she feels she's speaking the truth. To Brit and to herself.

'Now it's your turn!' Alicia says and Brit bites her lip.

'Oh, I don't know. Perhaps it's all going too fast.'

'Tell me more!' Alicia is so relieved that she doesn't have to talk about Patrick anymore that she milks all the information she can from Brit—who this Jukka character is, how they met, what he said, and what he's like.

'He sounds really nice,' Alicia says and squeezes her friend's hand across the table.

She casts her eyes over to the window and sees they are close to Sjoland. The tannoy comes alive with a crackle and the senior deckhand of the ferry asks all drivers to return to their cars.

Alicia gets up. 'Look, I've got to get back to work. But we have to have lunch or something.'

'Yes, we need a proper catch-up. Come to my place soon?' Brit scribbles an address on the back of a receipt and hands it to Alicia.

Alicia looks at the number of the building and her fears are confirmed. It seems Brit lives just one floor down from Patrick in the exact same block.

FOURTEEN

Patrick watches Alicia enter the newspaper office. She looks a little disheveled, he thinks. She's obviously been out in the snow storm, but where? The underground parking lot is available for the staff of *Ålandsbladet* and there's a direct internal lift straight to the office, so there is no need to walk outside.

'You OK?' Patrick asks when Alicia sits down opposite him, half concealed behind a bright blue screen that divides the desks in the open-plan office.

She gives him a quick glance, nods, and without saying a word begins typing.

Patrick pretends to be working, or interested in the preliminary layout of tomorrow's paper which has just been sent to him.

After his divorce, Kurt Eriksson, his former father-in-law, had made him news editor, a title that hadn't existed before. Kurt said it was so he 'wouldn't be a jobless embarrassment to the family.' But what can a news editor do when there is no news to report? Today, for example, his main task is to decide whether to lead with the local school Christmas drawing competitions or the slight delays to the ferry service due to weather conditions. How he aches for a proper story, a snow storm so severe that the island is cut off for days, for example. He didn't want anyone to be hurt, of course not, but oh, for proper news! After six months, he is so bored and frustrated that he can hardly wait till the end of December, when he can move back to Stockholm.

Patrick smiles to himself as he gazes at Alicia. He sees her turn around and peer at the glass cubicle. Noticing the empty chair of the editor, her eyes move toward Patrick. He can't help himself and grins, which he immediately realizes is a mistake. Alicia's face quickly returns to her screen. She lifts her fingers and begins to type furiously. Patrick sighs and pushes himself up from his chair.

Patrick knows how much it hurt Kurt to give him this job and therefore the chance to stay on the islands. Although nothing to do with Kurt, he had squirmed over Patrick's right to arrange set times to see the girls too. By that point, four months ago, Mia had been desperate to make the relationship with her lover official, so the family had accepted nearly every one of Patrick's demands. Now that he has decided to go back to Stockholm after all, he knows the family will be overjoyed. But he still has Christmas to get over. Perhaps there would be a big story, and he could leave the paper on a high. How sweet it would be to make Kurt Eriksson plead with him to stay on at *Ålandsbladet*.

Patrick decides to forget about his in-laws for a moment and find out what Alicia is up to. Perhaps she is following a story with an international slant that he would be able to sell worldwide? Something like the case of the oldest champagne in the world, which was found in the sea near Föglö a few years ago.

That would do nicely.

Convincing himself that his only motive is professional, he lifts his head and addresses her.

'The snow suits you.'

Alicia looks startled. She touches her hair, and tries to smooth it down.

That was too personal. The deal is: work chat only.

Patrick rubs his hands together and adds, trying to make the conversation sound general and impersonal, 'It's awful weather out there.'

'What do you want, Patrick?'

If looks could kill.

'Wow, steady on! What have I done?'

Alicia leans back on her office chair.

'Sorry, it's been a challenging day.'

'Care to tell me about it?' Patrick glances briefly around at the five other people in the office and nods in the direction of the glass cubicle.

Alicia's shoulders slump and suddenly she reminds him of his eldest daughter, who at the age of 10 is going on 15. When he was young, there was no such thing as a 'pre-teen.' Just like Sara, Alicia gets up slowly, and shuffles behind Patrick, making her reluctance clear.

FIFTEEN

'So, how are you?'

Alicia glares at Patrick. As the news editor, he can use the glass cubicle for private discussions. He's asked Alicia to sit on a chair next to the editor's vast leather one at the side of Harri's desk. She knows this area is less visible from the main office, but Alicia doesn't care if she's seen by the other reporters. Her relationship with Patrick is purely professional and as far as she knows no one at the newspaper knows about what happened the previous summer.

'What is this? Editorial control? By you?'

Patrick sits back and rubs his chin. Alicia sees that he's cut himself shaving again and tries to stop herself from smiling. It's as if the man is a teenager the way he can't shave properly. Like Stefan, she thinks fondly, remembering her son at the breakfast table, his skin covered with pieces of tissue stuck to the bleeding bits.

Her face must have betrayed a mood change, because Patrick leans over and suddenly takes her hands in his.

'I can't stop thinking about you.'

Alicia is taken aback but sits still, gazing at Patrick's strong fingers around her own. These fingers had ignited something animal in her last summer, when she couldn't get enough of him. She doesn't dare look up at him, fearing she will show that she is missing their physical closeness. She knows that if she gives in even a little bit they will be back in that vortex of passion, hurting every-body, including themselves, with their actions.

Without lifting her eyes to him, Alicia says, slowly and deliberately, 'Patrick, we agreed.'

But she's not allowed to finish her sentence before Patrick interrupts her.

'I know what we said, or rather, what you decided should happen in the future, but I am now divorced, Frida and the baby are doing well, and Liam is still in London.'

At the mention of Liam, Alicia looks at the blue eyes that made her wild with desire just a few months ago.

She says, 'But I am still married to him.'

Patrick inches closer with his leather chair. 'Do you love him?'

When Alicia says nothing, Patrick continues, 'Your silence speaks volumes, Alicia. Besides, how can you love a man who you never see? How many times in the last six months has he visited the islands to see you and his granddaughter? Two, three times?'

'He has a very important and demanding job. A surgeon can't just leave his patients,' Alicia says. She can hear her voice betray the doubts she herself has battled with since she decided to stay in Åland. She knows she will never want to go back to London, even though Liam pleads with her every time they see each other, as well as during their occasional video calls.

'They are more important than his wife and family?' Patrick says, releasing her hands. Alicia can see the contempt for Liam in Patrick's face.

'You don't understand,' Alicia says, moving her eyes back to her lap. She glances briefly toward the general office to see if anyone is paying attention to the two of them in the corner of the room. The staff are all sitting at the other end of the open-plan space, where they cannot see Patrick and Alicia, unless they move and openly stare at them. That's something, Alicia thinks and she gazes back at Patrick.

He's looking at the desk, deep in thought, it seems. He's wearing his customary white T-shirt, this time under a blue and white checked shirt. His jeans aren't ripped, but still reveal his strong thigh muscles. Alicia moves her eyes toward his arms where she can clearly make out his biceps. Suddenly an image of his body over hers comes to her mind and she suppresses a quick intake of breath.

Seeming to read her thoughts, he turns his head toward her again and, leaning over, puts his hands on the seat, either side of her thighs, his thumbs under her legs. His touch is burning into Alicia's flesh, sending currents through her muscles and into her center.

Suddenly she's being pulled into the corner of the office. Patrick is holding onto her, and pushing himself against her. He finds her mouth and his lips are soft and probing at first, then hot and demanding. His tongue finds hers and Alicia forgets where she is, or who she is, and just savors Patrick's touch, the taste of his lips, and the passion they ignite in her body. She abandons herself to Patrick's touch, his hands slipping inside her jumper, against her bare back, pulling at the front of her bra. When his fingers find her left nipple, a short yelp escapes Alicia's lips. With that, she wakes up from the trance Patrick has sent her into. Panting, she pulls away from his embrace and says, 'What are you doing?'

Patrick is also breathless. 'You drive me crazy. I can't resist you.

'You know how much you mean to me, Alicia,' he adds, more seriously now, his voice hoarse. Alicia can feel the hunger for her emanating from his body. All she wants to do is close the gap between them and let him fold her into his arms again. Involuntarily, she glances down and sees Patrick's jeans are straining at the front. Oh, my God, how she still desires this man! But she knows that giving into Patrick now is the wrong decision. She is a grandmother and needs to make sure Liam stays committed to Frida and little Anne Sofie. They are a family and families must stay together.

'No, Patrick, I can't.'

Alicia looks pleadingly at Patrick, who goes back to the editor's chair, staring at the computer screen.

When he doesn't say anything, or even look up at Alicia, she adds, 'You know the situation, Patrick.'

Now the man stands up again and his blue eyes meet Alicia's.

'No, frankly, I don't understand what the problem is. I wanted to tell you that I am moving back to Stockholm in the New Year. The apartment in Mariehamn will soon go on the market and I'm getting one in Södermalm. I'm going back to work for *Journalen*. Please say you'll come with me!'

Alicia can't believe her ears.

'Patrick, you know even if I could ...'

But he won't let her speak. He puts one finger over her lips. 'I know how you really feel about me. I don't need an answer now. But I will convince you to come. Stockholm isn't as far as London!'

Alicia shakes her head, but her mind is running wild.

'Look. Think about it,' Patrick says and gives her a quick kiss.

SIXTEEN

Alicia returns to her desk and tries to concentrate on researching the angry Russian driver. But it's difficult to find out anything about him. There aren't even images on Google that match the man she met earlier in Föglö.

She sighs and looks up at the glass cubicle where Patrick has remained after their earlier tête-à-tête.

Why does he have to be such a good kisser?

Alicia can't believe that in one second, a single moment, all the self-control she has been practicing over the last few months fell away. Just like that.

Does this mean I am in love with Patrick?

Surely not? Surely that was just her body reacting to being starved of intimacy, even if it is of her own volition?

Alicia resists the temptation to put her head in her hands. Instead she gets up. She gives a quick glance toward the Editor's glass cubicle, where Patrick is gazing at the computer screen. She slips quickly off her seat, pulling her coat from the back of her chair and grabbing her red bag, and then leaves the office.

The light outside is fading, even though it's just 4pm. Alicia makes her way through the Sittkoff shopping center and decides to stop at the Bagarstugan café on Lilla Torget. The snow storm has left the landscape virgin white. Christmas decorations hang from lampposts and criss-cross the street overhead. Put up for the traditional Christmas Market in early December, they stretch the length of Torggatan from Sittkoff's to the Market Square. Stars are strung through the bare trees growing in tubs along the pedestrianized part of the street, and there's a vast Christmas tree, decked with fairy lights and massive white baubles, in a small square at the end.

The little town is busy with last-minute shoppers, in spite of the freezing temperatures. Alicia sees from the digital display above the shopping center that it's -3°C. Not too bad, she thinks, and she pulls a woolly hat she found in her desk drawer down over her ears. Her hair is still a little damp from her excursion to Föglö. What a day she has already had! With the Russian, then meeting Brit, her oldest friend. It was so strange the way the years just fell away as they talked. She is pleased that her friend is considering a new relationship, despite being cheated on by her Italian boyfriend. And that she's now living in Åland permanently. Both of them back home at the same time.

Inside the warm café, she lets herself think about what

just happened in the newspaper office, and what Patrick said to her.

Patrick is moving to Stockholm!

Because she was so taken aback by the news, as well as the passionate kiss, and the invitation to move to the Swedish capital with him, she hadn't thought about how she will miss him. If, as she now suspects, her feelings for him are stronger than she realized, how would she cope with not seeing him every day? They have become good friends, confidants, even, in spite of the constant sexual tension between them—a frisson she has convinced herself is just playfulness, the remnants of what once was. After what had just happened, she knows that neither of them had got over the affair.

Alicia takes a sip of her large cup of coffee and wonders why her overwhelming feeling is one of pure happiness.

You know how much you mean to me, Alicia.

Patrick's words repeat themselves in her head and she feels like a teenager.

He loves me. He loves me.

She must admit that working in the same office, and often together on a story, has been difficult at times. She was the one who had insisted on being professional, rejecting any closeness instigated by Patrick. On occasion, if they were both leaning toward a computer screen, her long blonde hair nearly touching his head, she would catch his familiar scent, or see the stubble on his chin, and have the most overpowering desire to touch him. She would always pull away and sometimes get up and move away on some pretext or other. Did Patrick notice her emotional turmoil on these occasions?

At least she now knows how *he* feels about her. He wants to take her with him!

Pull yourself together! You have a family who depend on you.

She has always loved Stockholm, but she's made her life here on the islands now. There's no way she's going to move away from Anne Sofie. But living an uncomplicated life away from the small island community has suddenly become attractive. She has to admit to herself that she's still hung up on Patrick. But how much?

And what about Liam? What if Liam is planning to give up work and move to Åland after all? Her feelings toward her estranged husband (is that what he is?) are even more complicated than they are toward Patrick. She wishes she could decide what to do once and for all.

After accepting that Stefan was the baby's father, Liam's tenderness toward Frida took Alicia completely by surprise. It was as if her old Liam was back. She was certain that, with time, she'd be able to love him as she had done before Stefan's death.

No, her relationship with Liam had been on the rocks well before that. Over the months since they have been living in different countries, Alicia has come to realize that she fell out of love with him long before they lost their son. Even before she found out about his affair. At the time, when a 'friendly' acquaintance told her about Liam's 'indiscretion', she had been upset, but not really as devastated as she *should* have been. Thinking back, she can't remember when they grew apart. Perhaps it was after Liam decided he should sleep in the spare bedroom.

He had used the pretext of not wanting to disturb Alicia when he got home in the middle of the night after a particularly difficult operation. An occasional night away from Alicia's bed had gradually become the norm, and their lovemaking had become even more infrequent. Why hadn't Alicia protested? Or invited Liam back to their bed?

Alicia suspects there had been other women before the Polish nurse, but Liam had sworn she was the first and only one.

Alicia is brought back to the present by a tall young woman in a red and white checked apron, who is going around the small café clearing the tables. She picks up Alicia's empty cup and asks if she'd like anything else, another coffee or perhaps a cinnamon roll, but Alicia shakes her head. She checks her watch and realizes its nearly 5pm. Only five days till Christmas! She's forgotten to pick up the fish for gravlax. If it is to be ready for Christmas Eve, she and Hilda need to put it into the salt and dill marinade today. She picks up her woolly hat and bag and rushes out of the café.

SEVENTEEN

When Frida wakes up, her breasts are aching. They are painfully full with milk. It must be time for a feed, she thinks, looking at the baby monitor next to her. She sees that her daughter is awake. It's just before 6am and Anne Sofie is gurgling to herself, lifting up her long legs inside her pink and white sleep bag.

A gift from Alicia.

Frida tiptoes to the next room, where she has placed the white cot bought by Alicia at IKEA last summer. She opens the black-out curtains and turns around to see a sweet smile light up her daughter's face. As Frida lifts up her little baby girl, Anne Sofie starts making sucking sounds, smelling the milk on her mother.

'Let's just get you changed first, girly,' Frida says and carries Anne Sofie to the living room where she's set up a changing station against one of the walls. Alicia advised her to put it next to the cot, but Frida decided to leave it in the living room, where she spends most of her time with the baby.

She sighs as she thinks about Alicia. As she removes the soiled diaper from the baby, wipes her clean, and quickly replaces the soft cotton and plastic garment, she wonders how the first months of her baby's life would have been without Alicia.

Her cheeks redden when she thinks about the time and money Alicia has devoted to the baby—and her. Of course, Frida is grateful, but.

Frida makes herself comfortable and places Anne Sofie on her lap. The baby quickly finds the nipple Frida offers and starts sucking in steady, satisfying pulls. Frida relaxes her muscles: the relief is palpable. She looks down at the baby's eyes, firmly fixed on her own. She wonders— once again—what goes through that small brain while she feeds. Probably nothing, just pleasure.

How wonderful it must be to be so innocent and new!

Frida thinks over the last five months and to her rash decision to say something she knew was wrong. Why did she do it? Was she hormonally unbalanced?

She's heard of temporary insanity during pregnancy. The death of both Stefan in November, just as she'd found out about the baby, and then later in the summer, of her friend Daniel, who'd had an accident at sea, would surely have made anyone go a bit crazy? Losing someone you were so in love with, and then her best friend so soon after, had been a shock. And then her poor mother. Although that had been a relief for her mother, Frida is sure of it.

As she moves the baby from one breast to the other, Frida thinks how her mother would have loved little Anne Sofie, if she had known who the little baby was! When Frida introduced the baby to her grandmother, Sirpa had looked blankly at the small bundle in Frida's arms. By that stage, her mother had been asleep most of the time and didn't even recognize her own daughter, let alone a new grand-child. The staff at the care home had woken Sirpa to meet Anne Sofie, which meant she was groggy from sleep as well.

Frida would give anything to have that moment again. She would wait for as long as it took for her mother to have a lucid moment, something that still occasionally happened, even then. She's sure her mother would have recognized that the baby was the spitting image of her grandmother–her real grandmother that is. Instead, she left when the baby began to stir, telling the staff she needed to feed her. She'd been upset, still hormonal after the birth. She'd put the baby in her pram, and when she got back to her apartment, she had wept.

She hadn't realized it was the last time she would see her mother alive.

A day later, her mother fell asleep and never woke up again. The doctor said she'd had another massive stroke, but had assured Frida that she hadn't suffered.

Suddenly, a sadness overwhelms Frida. Tears run down her cheeks, landing on the baby's arms. She wipes them away and takes a deep breath. She needs to sort out her mother's affairs. If only she could have talked to her mother one more time, to clear her mind from the thick fog that had enveloped it for over a year now. Frida wanted to ask Sirpa so many questions about herself as a baby, about how she found bringing up a child on her own, about her father.

The day after her mother's death, when Frida was talking to the head of the home about funeral arrangements, a man approached her and handed over his card.

'Keith Karlsson, your mother's lawyer.'

Baby Anne Sofie was in a sling, snuggled up against Frida's breasts. She looked over to the *Solsidan* manager, who had just smiled and nodded to Mr Karlsson.

'I think we are all done here?' She touched Frida's arm and left the little room with its small sofa and two matching armchairs. Frida knew this was a space for bereaved and upset family members. She'd often seen people with their heads bent speaking with one of the carers or the manager there.

Anne Sofie gave a soft cooing sound, and Frida adjusted herself slightly, making sure the baby was comfortable, and that her small head was supported by the sling.

She looked across at Keith Karlsson, a man with thick gray hair, cut short into an American-style crewcut. He wore a suit with a shirt and tie and a large gold watch on his wrist. He was tan with tidy hands and nails as if he'd just had them manicured that morning. Which he might well have done.

'May I?' he said, indicating the seat the manager had just vacated.

Frida nodded. She couldn't understand how her

mother could afford the services of this wealthy looking lawyer. Or why she'd need someone like this anyway?

Frida had never before set eyes on him but Mr Karlsson seemed to know all about her.

'Please come and see me. We need to deal with your mother's affairs.'

EIGHTEEN

Mr Karlsson's offices are right in the center of town, on Torggatan. There's a small entrance next to the bank and stairs up to the third floor where a brass plaque on the door says *Karlsson & Co*.

Frida feels totally exhausted. Anne Sofie had refused to settle for a proper nap all morning. It wasn't until after her midday feed that the baby wanted to sleep. Just as it was time for Frida to come into town for this meeting.

The snow storm has left Mariehamn looking fresh and clean under a white blanket of snow. The afternoon is already turning into dusk, but the Christmas lights strung across Torggatan, and the decorations in the shops, make the center of town look magical.

Little Anne Sofie is now fast asleep in the sling, but Frida has had to drag herself into town, wrapping herself and the baby under layers and layers of clothing, rather than taking a well-deserved rest.

Frida nearly put this meeting off again, but she knew

she had to deal with her mother's affairs. It had been two months since her death and she keeps getting messages from Mr Karlsson's office. Besides, she has been living hand to mouth on state maternity pay and relying too heavily on Alicia and Liam's kindness. She has no idea how the rent on the apartment is paid for. She probably needs to transfer the rental agreement to herself. Unless that can't be done, in which case she needs to be rehoused by Mariehamn Council? She's ashamed of her incompetence when it comes to practical matters. It's as if during her pregnancy, and after Anne Sofie birth, she hasn't been able to think straight. Her mind doesn't have enough room to deal with money as well. Especially after her mother's death, nothing but Anne Sofie's well-being seemed to matter.

The lawyer opens the door immediately when Frida rings the bell. He smiles broadly at Frida, and when she reveals the bundle under her thick coat, gently removing Anne Sofie's woolly hat, he admires the sleeping child. Frida's heart melts a little when Mr Karlsson comments on the blonde curls and calls Anne Sofie 'an angel.'

Mr Karlsson ushers Frida into his office, which overlooks the streets below. At two o'clock, the town is busy with shoppers, not put off by the chilly temperatures and snow. Everyone is getting ready for Christmas, Frida thinks to herself.

In a weak moment, she had agreed to spend Christmas Eve with Alicia at Hilda and Uffe's house. She's determined to stay only one night. Of course, Alicia has insisted she should spend the whole holiday in Sjoland, but for now, Frida has managed to stay firm. Alicia could be quite insistent.

Frida sighs.

Since Anna Sofia's birth, her life hasn't been her own anymore. Of course, the baby's demands are paramount, but Frida hadn't counted on such strong interference from Stefan's family. Although his father, Liam, was rarely on the islands, preferring to stay and work in London, Alicia was more than enough on her own.

'We'd better get on with it, don't you think?' Mr Karlsson says, arousing Frida from her thoughts.

Frida nods.

'From my memory, babies have a knack of waking up at the most inconvenient moments,' Mr Karlsson adds as he opens a file on the desk. He hands it to Frida saying, 'Your mother's will.'

Frida is still surprised this wealthy man would know anything about her mother's affairs, let alone looking after babies, but she smiles and takes the folder from the lawyer.

She reads the legal text telling her that she, Frida Anttila, is her mother's sole beneficiary. But when she spots the final estimate of her mother's estate, she takes a quick intake of breath and puts her hand across her mouth.

The baby stirs against her body, and Frida tries to steady her breathing as she hands the folder back to Mr Karlsson. She places a palm on the sling and strokes Anne Sofie's back, trying to calm herself.

'I don't understand.'

'It's good news, my dear,' Mr Karlsson says, smiling broadly.

Frida tries to control her annoyance at the lawyer's patronizing attitude. She's a grown woman, a mother, and a grieving daughter! She may only be eighteen, but that means she is an adult and should be treated as such and not like some little school girl.

'Please explain,' she says, keeping her mouth straight and her voice cool.

Mr Karlsson's smile disappears, and he gives a brief cough.

'As I am sure you can ascertain, there are 998,525 Euros in your mother's savings account. On top of that, a regular sum of 5,000 is deposited to her current account each month.' The lawyer clears his throat once again, and continues. 'This monthly sum more than paid for the nursing home fees, the running costs on the property she owned and other incidentals. Nearly half of it was usually left over. I was instructed to transfer these sums into the savings account at the end of each month.'

Frida is stunned. She knows her mother's salary from Arkipelag wasn't anywhere near 5,000 Euros a month. Besides, since her fall and stroke, her mother wouldn't have been receiving anything apart from some sick pay at most. And nearly a million in savings! There is no way Sirpa would have been able to save that amount of money.

'You mentioned a property?'

'Yes, the one you are living in. Are there any others?'

Frida shakes her head and stares at the man.

While Frida listens in silence, Mr Karlsson tells her

that she is now a rich woman and won't need to worry about money, providing she takes investment advice.

'His, presumably', Frida thinks.

He hands her a pile of papers, including 'Ms Anttila's', as he calls Frida's mother, latest bank statements. As if to prove that the previous documents were correct.

'Who makes the monthly deposits?' Frida asks

The lawyer leans back in his chair. 'I'm afraid I can't divulge that information.'

'What? Why not?'

'Client confidentiality.'

'But I'm her daughter, surely if anyone, I am allowed to know this information.'

'I mean the other party.'

Frida narrows her eyes. 'You mean the person who pays in the money?'

The lawyer closes a folder he has been looking into. A copy of what he has given Frida, she supposes.

'I'm afraid I have other clients to attend to. Please let me know if you would like me to continue to look after your affairs. It would be a privilege to do so. Of course, there is no rush, after Christmas is fine. The process will take some time to go through. In the meantime, if you would like, I can transfer a sum, say 10,000 Euros, to your account?'

Frida gazes at the lawyer. The whole of this affair stinks to her. As does this man, his office, his gold watch, tan, and the money. But she can't believe her mother would be involved in something shady. She was a lowly waitress at Arkipelag, how can she have so much money stashed away? Where did she get it? Surely her mother hadn't been a criminal?

'Look, I've looked after your mother's affairs for over seventeen years. Christmas is coming. Please let me make it easier for you and the baby. Just let me have your bank details and the amount will be deposited to your account by tomorrow.'

Mr Karlsson is looking at Frida, waiting for her reply. When she isn't forthcoming, he sighs.

'Your mother had a benefactor. Someone she knew years ago who wanted to make her—and your—life easier. This person just wishes to remain anonymous. There is nothing unusual about that.'

'There is something usual about having nearly a million on a deposit account while working as a waitress, isn't there?'

The lawyer smiles, 'Your mother was an unusual person.'

NINETEEN

Discovering Sirpa Anttila was rich comes as a total shock to Frida. She's always been under the impression that the apartment they had shared, and in which Frida now lives with the baby, was rented and owned by Mariehamn council. She's never seen the bills, but her mother told her before she fell ill that all of it was taken care of by a direct debit.

Now Frida feels stupid that she hadn't looked into her mother's affairs while she was at the *Solsidan* home. Or confronted the manager about where the fees came from. She had been preoccupied with her own problems. The pregnancy, and grieving for Stefan and Daniel, as well as the worry about Alicia's sudden appearance in Mariehamn had distracted her.

'You don't have to worry about a thing,' Sirpa had told her the day Frida came back from Stockholm, where she had been studying for her Baccalaureate exams. Her mother was still in hospital then, with tubes attached to her hand and nostrils. Her voice was weak and croaky, and she looked thin and pale in her white hospital gown.

A week later, when Sirpa was brought back home, she had already become confused, forgetting to ask to go to the toilet and just wanting to stay in bed all day long. Frida cared for her mother at home for just over four weeks. An exhausting and awful time. Every night, Sirpa would soil the bedsheets, and occasionally during the day. She woke up many times each night, calling for Frida, and for someone with a Russian name. When Frida asked her mother who she was talking about, her mother's watery blue eyes would shoot up. 'No one you need worry about,' she'd mutter. Or she would grow hostile and angry, and shout at Frida to leave her alone.

Those weeks Frida tried to care for her mother were the hardest time of her life. Even harder than losing Stefan and Daniel. It was as if she was suddenly sharing her apartment—and her life—with someone else: a stranger. A stranger who would occasionally become her mother again, the quiet, kind woman whom Frida had known all her life. The mother who, when Frida was at the Gymnasium in Stockholm, would text her every day asking how she was, and always ending the message with, 'Don't forget I love you, my darling girl.'

The extent of her mother's drinking was a complete surprise to Frida too. During those awful four weeks at home, Sirpa insisted on having a bottle of vodka by her bedside, 'for nighttime emergencies.' When Frida tried to remove the bottle, her mother became angry and once even hit Frida across her legs.

When Frida read Sirpa's medical records, she found

that she'd been treated for various conditions 'indicative of high alcohol consumption.' She saw that there had been other hospital visits when Sirpa's alcohol levels had been sky high.

Of course, Frida knew her mother liked a drink or two. She worked in a restaurant, surrounded by alcohol and drinkers, after all. But she had no idea that her mother was an alcoholic.

It was a health visitor, an overweight woman, speaking with heavily accented Swedish who'd said it was time to move her mother to the *Solsidan* home. She was the same woman who had phoned the school in Stockholm and left a message about Sirpa's fall and stroke at the Arkipelag restaurant.

'She'll be well looked after at the home,' she'd said.

'What about the cost?' Frida had asked. She knew they were barely making ends meet with Sirpa's wages from waitressing. If Frida hadn't received a grant from the Åland Department of Education toward her fees, living costs, and travel to Stockholm, she'd never have been able to go to the Gymnasium.

But the woman just smiled and told Frida 'Not to worry, you will manage.'

When, after the first week, Frida had again asked the manager about the fees, the woman had looked at her computer screen and told Frida it was all taken care of. 'It comes from your mother's bank account by direct debit,' she had said.

How could Frida not think there was something strange going on when the manager made a similar comment about the funeral costs?

'It's all been taken care of. Your mother organized it all before she became confused,' the manager said and touched Frida's arm.

It takes Frida a full 24 hours to come to terms with what Mr Karlsson told her. She sends him an email with her bank details and an hour later, she sees the 10,000 Euros in her account. She's decided to enjoy the money–that's what her mother would have wanted, she's sure of it. She will think more about what to do after Christmas.

That night, Frida wakes suddenly. She gazes at the baby monitor, but Anne Sofie is fast asleep. Frida had been dreaming. In the dream, she'd been living in one of those beautiful villas on Solbacken, the most expensive real estate in Åland. She was sitting in a trendy wicker chair, attached to the ceiling, above a carpet of gold. She'd been rocking Anne Sofie wrapped in an expensive cashmere shawl. An older man had been humming and preparing some kind of food on a white kitchen island behind her. But she had woken up before she could see the man's face.

Frida shakes her head and looks at the clock next to her. It's just gone 12am. The baby will soon wake for her night feed, and as if roused by the power of her mind, the baby begins to murmur.

Now fully awake, waiting for the sounds from the monitor to become louder, the thought suddenly comes to Frida as clear as the virgin snow glittering outside her window. It must be her father who's been paying money into her mother's bank account.

Frida has no idea who the man is. Sirpa never mentioned him, just told Frida he was a foreign sailor who made her pregnant but never returned.

Now that Frida has discovered the money, she's not sure if she wants to know who this rich man is. He must have known about her mother's condition all along, as well as her exact whereabouts. He could have visited her at any time and got to know Frida. He obviously doesn't want anything to do with his family, so she doesn't want to know him either. She'll take the money, however. Why wouldn't she?

As long as she can remember, it's just been her and her mother. They didn't need anybody, but now, with a baby herself, Frida knows how much having the baby's father around would mean to her. Whatever the reason her own father didn't want to know her, it seems cruel to Frida.

Anne Sofie is now in full cry mode, so Frida gets up and goes to her. She decides to forget about the man–her father–and enjoy her newly acquired wealth.

TWENTY

Brit decides to use a bicycle with winter tires that Mia has offered her to get to the West Harbor from the apartment. The distance isn't that far, and with a push she could walk it, or she could drive, but she prefers the exercise that the bicycle provides. There is a walkway along the coast that is beautiful even in the freezing weather. The tires are amazingly good, making Brit enjoy the ride even more.

She also knows that the ruddy cheeks outside exercise gives her is flattering. She wants Jukka to see her at her best when she arrives for her second shift on MS *Sabrina*.

As soon as she has got off the bicycle and put it on the rack outside the terminal building, she sees Jukka driving past and parking his car. It's a sleek black Mercedes and Brit cannot help but be impressed.

She lingers on, pretending to have some trouble with the lock, when Jukka comes to stand very close to her.

'Can I help you with that?' Jukka says over her shoulder.

Brit pretends not to have seen him.

'Oh, hello!' she says and turns around. 'I'm fine,' she adds and smiles.

'Good to hear. Wouldn't want you to be a damsel in distress.' His eyes are wrinkled at the corners and she can see his warm breath turn to condensation. It's a bright, cold afternoon, with the sun low in the sky.

'Here she comes!' Jukka says and points at the horizon where a red dot can be seen moving toward them. He glances at a vast watch on his wrist and mutters, 'But where's MS *Diane*?'

For a moment they both gaze ahead, looking for signs of *Sabrina*'s sister ship in the wide shipping lane, which narrows as it gets further away and then divides in two. The right lane takes the ships to Sweden, the left to Finland. Suddenly, as the first red dot begins to take the shape of a ferry, another small object, like a speck of brick dust against the white ice, appears beyond MS *Sabrina*.

'Ah, there she is!' Jukka says and puts his hand on Brit's back. 'Let's get inside, out of this damn cold?'

Later, when Brit is on the ship, stationed at the door with the Second Mate, a young man in his twenties with a wide smile, ready to welcome day-trippers from *Sabrina*'s sister ship as well as those passengers embarking from Mariehamn, Brit can still feel Jukka's touch against her lower back. Even through the padded jacket, her jumper, a silky slip that she wore over her best bra today, his hand burned through to her skin.

During her first shift, she had found out that Jukka lived just outside Mariehamn. She'd also learned from Kerstin that he had been married before, information she'd delivered with a disapproving sneer.

'Ladies' man, that one,' she'd added.

That suits Brit just fine. She isn't after a serious relationship, just some fun to keep her mind off the Rat who broke her heart.

Getting ready at home, she was excited at the prospect of spending two nights in Jukka's company. She is planning to sneak into his cabin after her shift tonight, unless he makes a move first.

'I cannot be messing about at my age,' she'd told Alicia on the ferry back from seeing her dad.

'You never did,' Alicia said and giggled.

Brit smiles at the memory, nodding at a blond couple with two equally blond children walking through the sliding door of the ferry.

Spending the short ferry journey with her old friend had felt like being sixteen again, talking about the boys at school. Alicia never did anything about her infatuations (at school at least), whereas she usually took the first step. She'd lost her virginity in the back of a farm truck, after the school's year-end party. Brit knows that that particular boy, called Olaf, is now happily married with another girl in their class. They live somewhere in the suburbs outside Stockholm and have a string of kids, cats, and dogs. His Facebook page is full of pictures of outdoor activities, sailing in the summer and skiing in winter. The children look fat and unsmiling.

Lucky escape there.

Jukka has been busy all afternoon and early evening. There'd been a children's Christmas karaoke in the bar, which he'd been persuaded–by Brit–to judge. It wasn't something he usually got involved in but he just couldn't say no to her. Kerstin lifted her eyebrows when he passed her in the gangway on his way to the bar, but he ignored her. The ferry company was always encouraging him to be 'more visible' on the cruises. Apparently seeing the Captain about the ship made the passengers feel more secure. Plus, as one marketing woman put it, 'The Captain's visible presence is romantic.' As if he didn't have anything better to do!

But today, Brit's invitation was just too tempting. Unfortunately, there'd been a lot of people around so he couldn't ask her what he'd planned to.

Now, at 10pm, they should both be less busy. Most of the passengers had eaten already and the three à la carte restaurants and the self-service buffet are closed. There are three bars and a night club, but those are usually looked after by the nightshift and the two bar managers.

He knows Brit will either be in the staff quarters below deck or having something to eat in the canteen, but he doesn't want to go there. Too public, and he knows Kerstin is on duty today. He definitely does not want the old woman to see him making overtures to Brit. Would it be too forward to send Brit a message? He knows her mobile number, but only because he has access to her personal records. Perhaps it would be overstepping the mark. Yes, if he was planning to see her for personal reasons, but there is nothing to stop him from contacting her professionally.

Jukka gets out his phone and taps a message. He's on the bridge of the ship, sitting at the back while his First Mate, an experienced officer, is at the controls, keeping one eye on the ship's progress. Jukka trusts Oskar Brun implicitly. The younger man, who has a thick crop of brown hair, is only a year or so from attaining his Captain's stripes and Jukka will be sorry to see him go. They work well together and Oskar knows *Sabrina* as well as Jukka does, if not better.

It's pitch black outside. They're on the return leg back from Helsinki and are due to dock at Mariehamn just after 1am, so there are a few hours when Jukka can relax. With Brit, he hopes.

'I'm off, but you know where to find me?' Jukka says, addressing Oskar, and the young man nods in reply. There is no 'Aye, aye Captain,' from Oskar. The crew onboard rarely salute him, unless it's a very serious matter, or for show for the passengers. Marie Line, the shipping company, is 'a modern, progressive employer where each member of staff is valued.' Apparently this means that usual seafaring customs do not always need to be followed. He was still the commander of MS *Sabrina*, but it seems no one is required to show it anymore. Unless he is required to play a pantomime character for the passengers, that is.

Although a little weary, Jukka doesn't go straight to his cabin. Instead, he makes his way to the top deck, an area that is not visible from the bridge. It's bitterly cold as he steps outside, but there's not too much wind. The sky is filled with stars, a sight that nearly takes his breath away. He leans over the railing and lowers his eyes to the bow of the ship, checking that their course is a safe distance from the edge of the shipping lane and the thick ice. Which it is, of course.

This winter has turned very harsh. Only three weeks ago, the sea was cold and there was a thin layer of ice here and there, but there hadn't been any need for the ice-breakers. He inhales the night air and is about to turn back when he hears the door open behind him.

Brit sees Jukka's wide back as he rests his arms on the railing through the window of the door leading to the upper deck. The night sky is black against the white of his Captain's cap. Even from behind, he looks good in his uniform—tall, with a slim but muscular body. Brit cannot but wonder if Kerstin's assessment of him is correct: He could have any woman he so much as glances at.

Jukka isn't wearing an overcoat, but he doesn't look as if he's cold. Hot blooded, Brit thinks, and she almost laughs at her own corniness. Is she really so desperate that she needs to go to bed with Jukka, the first candidate since you-know-who, to prove that she's still attractive? Even though she only fancies him a tiny bit?

Don't think about it. You need to get back on the horse as soon as possible.

Luckily Brit has had the foresight to grab her long padded coat from her cabin. On her feet, she's wearing her high-heeled courts that she wears for work. She's not short by any means, but the added height gives her more authority over the staff, which is especially important in a new job. She looks down at the deck and wonders how slippery it is. Perhaps she should fake a fall, straight into Jukka's arms?

TWENTY-ONE

J ukka's cabin is on the top deck, behind a heavy locked door, which slides when he touches it with a keycard. They've taken a route through the crew quarters. When in the public areas, two women stopped Jukka to ask something obviously trivial that they already knew the answers to. The taller of the two wanted to know when they were arriving in Mariehamn, and the other asked what time they kept onboard, Swedish or Finnish? Both women were a bit older, perhaps in their fifties.

'These women want him too,' Brit thought to herself.

The taller, who was more forward, gave Brit a sideways glance as she stood next to Jukka, not too close, but near enough for it to seem they were together. Of course, if any staff saw them, they wouldn't have realized that there was anything going on. Or at least that's what Brit hoped, as she fixed her eyes on the two women.

Of course, nothing *was* going on—yet.

But Brit was delighted Jukka had initiated this meeting. A few moments ago, when Brit opened the door to the deck and Jukka saw her, he'd immediately smiled.

'You got my message?'

Brit nodded and took a couple of careful steps toward him, making them both laugh at the silliness of her shoes.

'You'd think I'd be a bit more sensible with my footwear. I've been working on ships for years!'

'Why don't we go somewhere warmer and more comfortable to talk?' Jukka said. His eyes were locked on hers, and although she was shivering under her warm coat, she could sense the heat inside her rise.

'Good idea.'

'What about my cabin? I could make you a proper coffee? I have a Nespresso machine,' Jukka said.

Brit knew exactly what she was agreeing to when she smiled and nodded. Jukka helped her back inside.

'Shall I show you the way?' Jukka said, removing his cap and smoothing his thick hair into place.

Inside his quarters, which include two rooms, Brit is speechless at the sight that greets her. In the lounge area, there's a sofa and two armchairs, a vast plasma TV screen, and angled rectangular portholes that almost cover one bulkhead. She can imagine what the view must be like in daytime. Now all she can see is blackness. Brit peers to her right, where a massive bed made up with pristine white sheets dominates the cabin area.

Jukka takes off his cap and coat and hangs them up in a small closet. He stretches out his hand and Brit lets him take her padded coat, which she's been carrying in her arms all the way through the ship.

Jukka loosens his tie and turns to Brit, who's still standing by the door, taking in the luxury of the Captain's accommodation. 'Please sit down, those heels must be killing you.' He gives her a wicked grin and Brit feels herself blush as his eyes travel from her shoes to her legs and up the length of her body to her eyes.

What's this? I don't blush!

'How do you take your coffee?' Jukka asks

'As strong as you can make it. Espresso, please, if you have some capsules for that?'

As she watches him stand over and operate the machine, Brit suddenly realizes why she is so drawn to this man. He's the spitting image of George Clooney! She better not tell him she can see a likeness to the dishy American actor she's been daydreaming about for years. 'Perhaps sometime in the future,' she thinks and smiles.

'What's so funny?' Jukka asks. He places a small cup on a low wooden table in front of her and comes to sit next to Brit on the sofa.

'Nothing,' she says, and she coyly crosses her legs. She's made sure her skirt is just short enough to show the lacy tops of her black thigh-highs.

Although Brit seems completely up for it, even teasing him with her body gestures, crossing her legs and smiling at him sweetly, never taking her eyes off him, Jukka is still not sure if he can risk making an advance. They are in his cabin, having coffee, to which she had willingly agreed.

How much clearer could she be, without actually uttering the words, that she wants him?

Yet.

Of course, he would like nothing better than to run his hands over those legs, touching the lace on her stocking tops, but what if he's misjudged the situation after all?

Again.

Brit has only just started at Marie Line. This is only her second shift on *Sabrina*. Wouldn't it be wiser–given his history–to just talk to her tonight, find out a little more about her and then, if, say, next time they are on shift together, go the whole way?

'So, tell me, how are you finding life back on the islands? I believe you have been working on the Caribbean Cruises for a few years now? Surely,' Jukka says, sweeping his hand out over the cabin, 'this must be a lot less glamorous. For a woman like you.'

Jukka couldn't stop himself from adding that last remark. As he says it, he feasts his eyes on Brit's perfect figure. Her eyes, which seem more aquamarine tonight, are sparkling and her skin dewy and glowing. Her legs are slim and long, and he can just make out the contours of a lacy black bra underneath a silky blouse.

Brit leans ever so slightly toward him and replies, 'On the contrary, I've never seen a more luxurious sleeping quarters.'

When she pronounces the word, 'sleeping' she does it slowly, deliberately articulating each syllable. Jukka thinks, I'm going to kiss her, but then checks himself just in time and instead, gives a small cough. He adjusts his seating position a little, so that he's a fraction farther away from the woman. And temptation.

'Really,' he says, trying to keep his voice deep and calm.

'Uh, huh.' Brit replies. It's as though she's purring at him. How is he going to get out of this situation, that he himself has created, without offending her? Or worse, without her ever wanting to set eyes on him or his cabin ever again?

'Look, Brit, I really like you.'

Again Jukka hesitates. Even that could be misconstrued to be too forward and personal. 'I mean you seem to have fitted in very well.'

Just as he is thinking what on earth he has to do or say to resolve the situation, his intercom buzzes. He takes a quick look at the screen and says, 'I'm sorry, I'm needed on the bridge.'

TWENTY-TWO

Brit wakes up with an inexplicable headache. She's only had about four hours' sleep, if that, but she's well used to doing long shifts with little rest in between. So it's not that. She looks at the screen of her phone and sees it's gone half past four. If she doesn't get a move on, she will be late for the start of 'Sea Breakfast' at 5.30am. Most of the passengers, she knows, will be bleary eyed, but it doesn't do for the staff to look hungover—especially the restaurant manager. She hadn't had a drop to drink last night, but her sleep was disturbed by her encounter with Jukka.

The man was blowing hot and cold on her and she didn't understand why. The electricity between them can't just be in her imagination, can it?

As Brit takes a swift shower in the small cubicle in her cabin, she remembers how, when they were sitting in Jukka's cabin, she thought he was going to lean over and kiss her, stopping himself just before it happened. What is wrong with him? Or is it her? Doesn't he fancy her after all?

Brit dries herself and puts on a new white uniform blouse, although it's cotton this time, rather than the silky number she wore last night. She was relieved to discover on her first day that the Marie Line crew could wear their own blouses and (black) shoes as long as they donned the company uniform jacket and skirt (or trousers, but Brit prefers a skirt). This gives her the opportunity to feel sexy, even at work. Besides, she's learned over the years that the shirts provided are often made out of scratchy polyester, which easily makes your armpits smell foul.

Surprised by the number of passengers who've booked for breakfast, Brit sets about inspecting the buffet, and makes sure that everyone who is supposed to be on duty has got out of their bunks. She makes a quick round of the galley and sees all is in order

It's now quarter past five and there's already a small line outside the glazed doors that lead to the large restaurant. Kerstin is on Maitre'D duty with a junior member of staff—a young dark-haired woman who looks a bit frightened. Brit nods to the two women standing with their backs to the locked doors, and they let in the first passengers. She stands to one side and smiles at the couple who are first in the line. And then she sees him, Jukka, hovering behind the passengers, gazing at her. He touches his cap as if in salute and Brit cannot help but beam at him.

Jukka is on the other side of the door, seemingly in no

hurry to enter the restaurant. The passengers are wary of him, leaving an empty circle around the Captain.

No flirtatious ladies this morning.

As is the custom, there is a Captain's table in every restaurant on the ship. It's usually the best table, with the most uninterrupted view of the sea, and only given to passengers if the Captain explicitly lets the staff know that he will not be eating there.

The space reserved for Jukka at the Buffet Restaurant (the only one of the four eating places onboard that opens for breakfast) is no exception. Brit now goes over to the table to ensure it's laid out correctly and that there is a 'Captain's Table' sign on it. It's covered with a white linen cloth and set for six people, in front of two large windows. The sun is far from rising, but there is a faint light on the horizon and Brit can see the outlines of the small islands of the Helsinki archipelago they are sailing through.

She's startled by Jukka's voice behind her, 'Won't you join me for breakfast?'

Brit turns around, and gives him one of her most charming smiles. 'Is that an order, Sir?'

Jukka laughs. 'No one even salutes me on this ship. But if you like, let's say I need to discuss something with you.'

Brit glances behind her, at the staff at the door. Kerstin is gazing at them. She's certainly clocked that they are having a light-hearted conversation even though she couldn't possibly hear what they are saying. She leans toward her colleague and says something. About her and Jukka, Brit is pretty certain.

Let them gossip away.

'In that case, I'd love to,' she says.

'So what was it you wanted to talk to me about?' Brit says after they have ordered their breakfast from a tall male waiter. Brit couldn't remember his name and had to ask him. She finds out that Olli has a stutter, and has only been a member of MS *Sabrina* crew for a few months. Although the breakfast is self-service, the Captain is given table service. Brit wonders why Kerstin, who is the most senior after herself, didn't come and look after them, but decided not to challenge her this time, in spite of the clear snub. Besides, Olli seemed perfectly competent, although terribly nervous, in his duties. In a way, Brit was glad they were not confronted by Kerstin's lopsided, insincere smile.

Jukka sets his eyes on Brit's and pushes his hand forward on the table, nearly touching her fingers, but then thinks better of it and retracts it, opening his linen napkin and placing it in his lap instead.

'I wanted to apologize for last night. I'm afraid there was an incident.'

'Really, what happened?' Although Brit has been bristling over the previous evening's events all night and morning, she's intrigued by what could have happened onboard that she hasn't yet found out about.

'We thought we had a jumper, but it turned out to be a prank.'

'How awful!' Brit is truly horrified. She knows that there have been suicides on the ferries between Finland and Sweden, but she hasn't heard of any for a long while. Perhaps they don't get reported?

'Yes, a YouTuber thought it'd be a good idea to film himself climbing the railings on deck 7. He jumped down to the level below, and it looked like he'd perished, so they called me in. Luckily, the guy is OK, although it could have gone very badly indeed for him.'

Olli interrupts their conversation with a plate of salmon and scrambled eggs for two, plus a steaming pot of coffee.

'I hope you confiscated the video?'

Jukka put his knife and fork down, swallowing a piece of salmon. 'Unfortunately, he managed to post it online before we got to him. I gave him a good talking to, but not sure if it did any good. The company lawyers will deal with it all now.'

He gazes intently at Brit and adds, 'I was quite mad at him. Especially as I had completely different plans for last night.'

TWENTY-THREE

Hilda is so bored. At first after they closed the fashion boutique, the relief she felt was enormous. It was as if a nightmare had ended, and at last she was able to sleep at night, and even have the occasional lie-in in the mornings if she wished. And she didn't have to make up any more stories for Uffe and Alicia about how many clients she'd served on any given day, or how many garments she'd sold.

On so many days she'd sit in that shop, watching the clock on the wall of the bank opposite, visible through the tall windows overlooking the street. The bank was always busy, people going in and out, staff staring at their screens, tapping away and occasionally listening to a client sitting in a chair on the other side of the desk. Hilda could only see the back of the person, but the bank clerk would have their head bent, and nod occasionally. None of those clients would ever cross the road and venture into her shop. Even people who knew her or Uffe—everyone on the islands knew her husband—only waved a greeting, making themselves look busy so they didn't have to come in and spend some of the money they'd just pulled out of their bank accounts.

But now she even misses those disingenuous so-called friends. And she misses the thrill of going to fashion shows in Milan, Paris, and Stockholm. She never attended the main events, that's true, but the buzz of the lower tier shows was enough to make her feel alive. Making decisions on what might sell in her small shop in Mariehamn, how daring she could afford to be, was always such a boost to her confidence. To think that she, a poor Finnish girl, who had hardly been able to pass her maths exams at the Kallio Lyceum at the age of sixteen, was now making calculations in her head about wholesale and retail prices and profit margins?

'For you, marrying a man who can look after you is the best option in life,' was what everyone had said, from her mother and father to her teachers. The general opinion was that she had no talent for study, but thank goodness she had her looks.

When she had to tell Uffe that she'd only been able to keep the shop going because of the loan she'd taken out with the Russian, Alexander Dudnikov, he was furious at first, but eventually he agreed to pay off the debt. To Hilda's horror, this had doubled in the few months since she'd taken the loan.

'What about the payments I made?' she asked Uffe. But he just shook his head.

'Promise me you will never have anything to do with

that man ever again?' he said, and she gladly gave a vow. Dudnikov was clearly a crook, and his henchmen were terrible thugs. Goodness knows what kind of criminal organization he ran. What they did on the island, Hilda could only imagine. Drugs, people trafficking, money laundering, and whatever else was illegal. Uffe had told her that he met Dudnikov through one of his old friends, someone he occasionally met for a beer in Mariehamn.

'He begged me to give a job to a laborer, who'd had to flee his own country. I thought he was a good guy,' he said.

When the Russian popped into Hilda's shop a few days later, she didn't think anything of it. The summer before had been a particularly slow June and July, and Hilda dreaded having to tell Uffe how much she owed the bank opposite. The clothes she'd bought in the shows were all hanging on the rails, stuffed to bursting point. She'd calculated that even if she put the stock on a half-price sale, she would still not pay off the loan.

Dudnikov had been a savior. On that first day, he'd bought so much stock—he told Hilda he had a large family, 'A lot of sisters, cousins, and aunts'—that Hilda thought she might even survive until the next season. Two days after that the Russian was back.

'My girls love your style,' he said and smiled broadly. Hilda noticed a gold filling at the back of his mouth and thought, 'How predictable,' but she forced herself to like the man. He was her only hope. All through spring, Dudnikov came into her shop and bought outfit after outfit. At the end of May, he said, 'I your only customer?' He had an accent, and his Swedish was far from perfect, but up till then, he'd been pleasant enough. Now his voice sounded harsh, his accent and demeanor, she decided, were more Russian.

All through her childhood, Hilda had been told never to trust a Russian. Her father had fought the Russians in Karelia, and her mother blamed his alcoholism and eventual death for the mental scars he'd received fighting the Soviets in the Winter War. When her father was out drinking at the weekends—he managed to hold down a job at the railways during the week—her mother would shout 'Don't trust the Russians!' at the grainy black and white television whenever she saw Kekkonen, the Finnish president, shaking hands with the Russian dictators—first Khrushchev, then Brezhnev.

Of course, now, Russians were everywhere. They had money and everyone wanted their custom. Gone were the rare vodka-smelling tourists of her youth, with yellowing teeth, bad crewcuts, and unfashionable clothing. The modern Russians wore Gucci and Louis Vuitton.

In the shop that day, Hilda had laughed nervously at Dudnikov, 'No, not at all.'

The truth was, during the days when the Russian wasn't in, Hilda sold one or two items at most. Without Dudnikov, she would have had to go to Uffe for money weeks ago.

The Russian had smiled and taken a step closer to Hilda. She had been forced to lean against a rail of discounted summer jumpers. They were striped Musto sailing pullovers, which she didn't usually stock, but she'd hoped they might bring a new set of clients into the shop.

She'd not sold one. Not even Dudnikov had touched them.

The Russian had made her an offer. He liked the shop, he said, and he wanted Hilda to continue. 'Perhaps I help a little with cashflow, yes?'

Oh, how Hilda now wishes, she'd been brave and told Uffe about the losses the shop was making. But over the twenty-four hours Dudnikov had given her to 'think it over,' she had calculated she would be able to pay back the loan—if the Russian carried on spending 500 Euros per week, as he had been doing, and began telling his wealthy Russian friends about her shop. Being in business meant you had take risks, she'd thought. But, of course, after he'd given her the money in a brown paper envelope (a loan in cash should have rung alarm bells!), the Russian stopped coming, and Hilda was back to long days watching the bank customers coming and going right past her shop.

The 20,000 Euros Hilda ended up owing Dudnikov was a vast amount. Uffe had to sell a piece of land he owned two fields away from his farm.

'It overlooks the sea and I always hoped we might build our own place there for retirement,' Uffe said and that made Hilda cry.

When they went to the bank to withdraw the money so that they could give Dudnikov his cash in a brown envelope, Hilda glanced over to the shop, which was being refitted. 'Barber Shop opening here soon,' said the notice on the door. She wondered if there was anyone inside, looking out at the two of them as they sat opposite the bank clerk. Someone worrying about their business, just as she had done. Most likely not, Hilda decided, turning her head back toward the woman, who, it transpired, had been in the same class as Uffe at junior school. Hilda hoped their lie about why they needed the money in cash–to buy a boat from a Finn on the mainland—was accepted by the woman, but it all seemed to be OK. She smiled at Uffe and Hilda as she counted the notes in front of them.

'I hope you are happy with your new boat!' the woman, who was wearing large black-framed glasses, said.

Hilda glanced nervously at her husband. 'I'm sure we will,' he said, returning the woman's smile. Hilda took a deep breath.

Uffe made the payment to Dudnikov alone.

'I want to see the whites of his eyes when I repay him. I don't want any comeback from that man.'

Hilda was glad; she didn't want to see the Russian ever again.

That was last August, over four months ago. Since then, they hadn't heard a word from Dudnikov. Until yesterday. Or was that man really Alexander Dudnikov, and had he really tried to run them off the road? The way Uffe reacted and didn't want to talk about it frightened Hilda all over again.

Hilda gets up and decides not to think about the Russian. Not today. Christmas is nearly here and she still has so much to do.

She reaches for her telephone and sends a message to her daughter.

'Don't forget the salmon!'

She gets up and climbs the steps to the attic where, in the back of the wardrobe, she finds a box of tree decorations. Some of them look a bit worn out, but she knows Alicia will want everything to be just as it was before, so she will resist an impulse to buy a new set from a shop selling stylish homeware that has just opened in town. Putting aside all the old candleholders, Hilda carefully untangles the silver-colored tinsel and checks that the ancient baubles are all intact. She then counts the number of candles left over from last year; there are enough for the first lighting of the tree.

She can't wait to see what little Anne Sofie thinks of the tree. She remembers as if it was yesterday Stefan's bright eyes when he saw it for the first time. A tear falls down Hilda's cheek and she wipes it away.

Stop being so sentimental. I won't have it from others, so I cannot succumb to it myself.

TWENTY-FOUR

'Did you get the dill?'

'Yes, and more salt, just in case,' Alicia says, giving her mother a quick hug.

The two women begin working on the fish. Hilda tuts as she runs her hand across the two fillets laid out on the kitchen counter.

'So many bones left. You'd better get the fish tweezers and get them all out. *Så slarvigt!*'

Alicia smiles at her mother's words. She thinks everyone else is lazy and careless, and most of the service you get in shops is shoddy these days.

'I know the fishmongers aren't up to your standard, but they were really busy. Just as well you ordered the fish, they'd run out,' she says and puts her arms around Hilda briefly.

Hilda straightens her back and Alicia smiles. Her mother is a formidable woman but the loss of her shop has taken some of the sparkle and fight that Alicia has come to love and dread in equal measure out of her eyes.

She knows the prospect of having everyone here to celebrate Christmas has made her mother happy. It's given her something to arrange and look forward to.

'Guess who I bumped into the other day?' Alicia says as she starts to remove bones from the fish fillets.

Hilda leaves Alicia alone in the kitchen to go and tell Uffe who, as usual, is sitting in his office across the yard, about the return to the islands of Alicia's old friend. Alone with the fish, Alicia suddenly thinks back to the previous Christmas, which they had been planning to celebrate with Hilda and Uffe in London. They were going to have the traditional Christmas Eve supper-a large roast ham, vegetable bakes, meatballs, marinated herring-the peculiar mixture of Finnish and Swedish traditions that the islanders adhered to. On Christmas Day, they'd have a British Christmas with turkey and all the trimmings. She remembers how Stefan hated turkey, and would always have leftover ham from Christmas Eve instead.

Last year, Hilda and Uffe journeyed to London weeks earlier in late November. Instead of celebrating Christmas, they attended Stefan's funeral. Hilda wanted to stay for the whole of December, until the New Year, but Alicia couldn't bear the thought of having everyone assembled around the Christmas table without Stefan. She wanted to forget that the holidays were coming. She wanted to forget everything and just sleep.

And sleep she had. Liam had administered various pills that allowed her to rest and feel detached from the world.

In the end, Liam booked them into a hotel in the center of town for Christmas. She didn't want to be among the strangers in the dining room, eating the stupidly expensive lunch, or listening to the other, happy, laughing, diners cheerfully wish each other Happy Christmas. And the weather was awful, with cold drizzle falling on both days. Walking along the cold streets, they had to duck into pubs, where the other customers were in the same high spirits as the hotel guests they'd tried to escape. On Boxing Day, in spite of the rain, they walked along the South Bank of the Thames to visit the seasonal outdoor market. But when she looked into the dark, fast-flowing river, Alicia had yearned to be there on her own. She wanted to walk across the brightly-lit Waterloo Bridge and jump into the Thames. But she knew Liam would stop her.

Those dark thoughts frightened her and the next working day she contacted Connie, her grief counsellor, to book an emergency session. Alicia shudders at the memory now and decides that this coming Christmas will be better. Much, much better. She'll make sure of it.

Breathe and come back to the present.

Alicia removes the fish bones one by one, and arranges the sugar and salt mixture, followed by the cut herbs, on top of the salmon fillets. She's closely supervised by her mother, back from Uffe's office across the yard. Hilda makes the final adjustments to the salmon.

'We'll look at it tomorrow and turn it over the day before Christmas Eve. Now, how about a glass of mulled wine? I've got the special edition *Blossa Glögg*. It tastes like limoncello this year!' Hilda shows Alicia a yellow bottle.

Alicia glances at the large clock on the other side of the kitchen wall. It's just coming up to five o'clock, but she nods to her mother, 'Why not?'

Over the past six months, Alicia has been trying to get used to the different drinking times—or lack of them—on the islands. With Liam in London, they had kept to strict times. Nothing until 6pm on weekdays, and only the occasional glass of wine at lunch on the weekends. She'd forgotten it was a British custom based on the old pub opening times, but after nearly twenty years in the UK, it was hard for her to get used to being offered an alcoholic drink at all hours of the day.

She's also worried about her mother's drinking. There isn't a day when Hilda doesn't have a tipple, be it a glass of beer or wine. Alicia hasn't seen her mother actually drunk, not more than a little tipsy on special occasions such as a meal when Liam is visiting from London, but there's rarely a time when Hilda doesn't have a glass of wine in her hand.

Alicia usually refuses a drink when her mother offers one, because she doesn't want to encourage any more alcohol consumption. But today, it's nearly Christmas, and after the day she's had—being nearly driven off the road by that unpleasant Russian, meeting her old friend, and then kissed and offered a new life by Patrick—she needs a drink herself.

After they've wrapped the marinated fish up and placed it

under some weights on the bottom shelf of the refrigerator, Alicia and Hilda sit down at the kitchen table with their glasses of mulled wine, *glögg*. Hilda looks at two pieces of paper, one covered with Christmas menus and the other a shopping list, with some items crossed out and more added, some in black ink, and some in blue and red.

'I think we'll invite Rolf and Brit over for Christmas, what do you say?' Hilda asks. 'Uffe thinks it's a brilliant idea,' she adds.

Alicia smiles, 'Really?' She doubts her stepfather put it quite like that.

'Yes, Rolf is quite frail and on his own, so I think it's perfect. There's enough room for them to stay over. If Liam and you can stay in the sauna cottage?' Hilda gives Alicia a careful glance.

'Yes, that's fine,' Alicia says quickly. Her mother hadn't commented on the sleeping arrangements during Liam's previous visits in the fall. This is uncharacteristic, but Alicia is grateful that her mother hasn't interfered.

'Now, tomorrow I will fetch the turkey from *Kantarellen*, unless you're in town? What do you think we should get for little Anne Sofie?' her mother continues.

'You sure we want to do the British Christmas as well? Isn't it just too much this year, with so many mouths to feed?'

Hilda takes a large swig out of her glass and goes around to the stove, where she's heated the *glögg* in her traditional copper pan, to pour some more for herself and to top up Alicia's glass, although she's only had time to take a sip. Hilda uses little silver spoons resting in a pair of a small decorative pots to add the traditional slivered almonds and raisins to her mulled wine.

'You know, I wasn't sure if these would go with this year's special edition wine, but they do, don't they?'

She looks up at Alicia and smiles.

'Don't change the subject. It's just too much. There's going to be, what, eight of us, including Brit and her father, who you really don't need to invite, you know!'

Hilda places her hand on Alicia's. 'I think it's perfect to have a full house this Christmas, don't you?'

TWENTY-FIVE

As soon as Hilda heard that Brit Svensson was back on the islands, she had the idea of inviting the girl and her father, Rolf, whom Uffe knew way back in school, to celebrate Christmas with them.

She now looks at her daughter, sitting at the kitchen table, inspecting Hilda's long Christmas list. She's got her mussed blonde hair in a bun, which highlights her angular face, where her weight loss shows the most. Her cheek bones are high and there are some fine lines around her pretty pale eyes. It's been a terrible year for her, and Hilda knows Christmas without Stefan will be challenging for Alicia, as it will be for all of them. Hilda will make sure the festivities go smoothly. The more people there are, and the less like a family occasion it is, the better Alicia will be able to cope.

Suddenly her daughter lifts her face up to Hilda. 'Mom, that Russian that you nearly collided with. Do you know him?'

Hilda's eyebrows shoot up. She curses herself for

making the mistake of telling Alicia that they recognized the driver of the Cherokee on their way back from the airport. She'd had too many miniature gin and tonics on the flight and wasn't thinking straight. Uffe was so angry with her that night. Even then, he wouldn't say why Dudnikov did it, though.

'It's nothing for you to concern yourself with,' he said and turned over in bed.

Hilda can now feel a faint blush rising her cheeks.

'No, of course not. Whatever gave you that idea?'

She can see her daughter knows she is lying, but can't challenge her. Or doesn't want to, perhaps?

'A man tried to run me off the road and I think it's the same Russian.'

'What? Are you alright?' Hilda takes Alicia's hands in her own. She glances down at her empty glass. She's finished her second glass of *glögg*. She should have added a slug of vodka to it, but she knows Alicia would have declined and then she would have looked like some kind of alcoholic. Which she isn't, of course.

Suddenly she can't take the lying anymore. She releases Alicia and covers her head with her hands instead. Alicia gets up and puts her arms around her.

'Tell me what's going on?'

Hilda can feel the strands of her daughter's blonde hair against her fingers, but she can't get the words out. The whole affair with that monster is so awful, and she's been so stupid, she really can't bring herself to tell Alicia.

'It's, it's nothing,' she manages to utter.

Alicia lowers herself to her knees and gently pulls her hands away. She peers at Hilda's face. 'This doesn't look like nothing,' she says gently. 'You can tell me. I might even be able to help.'

Hilda gazes at her daughter's face. She can now see the lines that weren't there twelve months ago more clearly, around her mouth and on her forehead. Alicia doesn't need any other worries, she tells herself, but at the same time Hilda is so tired of the secrets she's been keeping.

Hilda digs a tissue from the pocket of her Christmas-themed apron and dries her eyes and blows her nose.

Her mother is buying time and Alicia knows it. So she waits, perched next to the older woman. Eventually, after Hilda has had a good wipe of her face and blown her nose again, she inhales and exhales through her nose. 'It's all about money and my stupidity, really.'

TWENTY-SIX

The flight to Mariehamn is delayed by a further hour and Liam swears under his breath. He has Christmas off, but doesn't want to spend any more time in an airport than he has to. Truth be told, he's not a good traveler. He gets seasick on ferries and uneasy before a flight. The trip he's just taken from London to Helsinki was fairly uneventful until they began to descend. The captain informed the passengers that there was a snowstorm over southern Finland, but that they were going to attempt to land as usual.

Attempt to land!?

Luckily, Liam now travels in business class and the Finnair staff were understanding of his need for an additional double whisky to cope with these new circumstances. And they made it down without incident, but that doesn't do anything to allay his fears about the next leg of his journey. In another twenty minutes he's due to board a much smaller plane that will take him back in the direction he's come from, back over the Baltic toward the Åland islands.

Liam sips his drink–he's switched to gin and tonic–in the business lounge and thinks about his complicated life. Only twelve months ago, he was fairly happy with his lot. He loved his work as a respected surgeon at St Mary's Hospital in St John's Wood, North London. He was seeing another woman, but he still loved Alicia. He was close to finishing it with Ewa, the Polish nurse with the red lips and soft, willing body, when the worst happened. Alicia and Liam's wonderful, talented, beautiful boy, went out on his moped on a frosty night with icy roads and ended up hitting a wall. Not to have been able to live his life, to be killed even before he reached adulthood, is the cruelest fate. And Liam has to live with that. As well as the knowledge that it was he who persuaded Alicia that Stefan was sufficiently responsible to own and ride a bike at the age of seventeen. As if having an affair with another woman wasn't bad enough, Liam also carried the guilt of being responsible for the death of his own son, denying his wife the pleasure of seeing her child grow into a man.

Liam finishes his drink and goes to the bar to pour another one.

On his way back to his seat, he sees that the flight is at last boarding, so he downs the contents of the glass in one and makes his way toward the gate.

While he tries to ignore the bumpy ride back over the Baltic, he thinks about the surprise grandparenthood he and Alicia are now experiencing. Frida is a strange girl, with her rainbow colored hair and tattoos, but she has proved to be a good mother. There is no doubt that Anne Sofie is the most beautiful, thriving baby girl he's ever set eyes on. And it's clear the birth of a granddaughter, as well as the close friendship she shares with Frida has given Alicia a new reason to live. Without those two, Alicia would no doubt have returned to London by now, and possibly found some other way to cope. Perhaps by involving herself in some of the charities that he supports?

But, seriously, Liam can't see Alicia hosting charity galas or organizing a bunch of women to raise money for worthwhile causes. In the months after Stefan's death, when she surfaced from the depths of her grief, she would have left him if she'd stayed in London, there's no doubt in Liam's mind about that. There'd be another man—just look how quickly that arrogant Swedish reporter had lured her into his bed. But in the end she chose her husband, after Liam had made it clear how much he loved her and how sorry he was about his past actions. He didn't lie when he said Ewa meant nothing to him—it was just the sex.

Don't think about her.

Alicia and Liam are still not on those kinds of terms, which is making Liam crabby, but he knows he has to give her time. He needs to convince her to come back to London, where their marriage will have a fighting chance. This is why he's done what he has done. He thinks about the report emailed to him yesterday. At first, when he saw the results, he was jubilant. It was exactly what he had suspected from the very beginning, and it would give Alicia good reason to come home to the UK. But now, when the moment is nearly here, when he has to share the news with Alicia, he's beginning to doubt his own reasoning. To him, back in London that same morning, it had seemed clear. If Anne Sofie isn't their granddaughter, there is no reason for Alicia to stay on the islands. But what if Alicia feels differently?

Liam shakes his head—no, this is just his own fear of flying making him draw these irrational conclusions. Of course Alicia will see sense. Liam thinks he needs to be ready for the anger she will no doubt feel toward Frida. Having considered it carefully, Liam doesn't think she has led them to the wrong conclusion regarding the baby's paternity on purpose. No, he's sure she *thought*—even wished—Stefan was the father. It's clear that the girl was in love with their son, but sadly for her, the baby is somebody else's. The DNA test cannot be refuted: it's as clear as day that Anne Sofie is not the daughter of Alicia and Liam's dead son.

When Liam finally steps out of the plane at the small airport in Mariehamn, he spots Alicia standing behind the wire fence, smiling and waving. How he deserves this woman's love—or even friendship (because he's not sure she still does love him) he doesn't know. Dusk has fallen while he's been in the air, making the falling snowflakes quite pretty. He must learn to love this place. Everything would be so much simpler if he did.

'Good flight?' Alicia asks and brushes his chin with her lips.

Liam, possibly spurred on by the amount of alcohol

he has drunk during the long journey, takes his wife into his arms and pushes his lips onto hers. For a moment, Alicia doesn't react, but then she pushes him gently away.

'Long wait in Helsinki?' she says and grins at him. 'C'mon let's get you home. Hilda is waiting with your favorite reindeer steak and a chanterelle sauce.'

Liam sets his suitcase inside the trunk of the old Volvo and sits next to Alicia. He grins and squeezes her thigh.

Alicia looks at his hand. 'Sorry,' he says, 'I've had a few, but it isn't just that. I've missed you. And you look so good in that outfit. Those jeans,' he says, slurring slightly.

Alicia smiles sweetly at him and removes the hand from her lap.

'Alright, let's get going, eh?'

TWENTY-SEVEN

Alicia cannot stop thinking about Patrick and the taste of his lips. Here she is, sitting in the car with her husband, obsessing about another man. The kissing in the office released something inside Alicia and all she wants to do is to dump Liam in Sjoland, turn around, and go to Patrick. But, of course, she won't do that. Especially now she knows about Dudnikov. She needs to keep her family together, she needs to protect them from the Russian. As soon as she's at work, she will find out where the man is, and do some serious research into his illegal activities. She'll hand all the information to Ebba rather than write about it for the paper. Which is another reason why she needs to keep away from Patrick. He would love a juicy criminal story like this, but Alicia wants the man caught. Her journalistic ambitions must be put aside for the safety of her family.

'How have you been?' Liam says. He's looking at her across the darkened car, but Alicia stares straight ahead.

'Fine,' she replies and increases the speed.

'Don't be like that,' Liam says and stretches his hand toward Alicia once more, but she prevents another squeeze of her thigh by touching the gearshift between them.

'Sorry,' Alicia says and tries to smile at Liam. 'It's been a busy day.'

Liam sighs heavily and leans back in his seat, looking out into the darkness.

'There's a lot of snow,' he says.

TWENTY-EIGHT

'You've done what?' Alicia's pale eyes are almost black. While she has been reading the email on Liam's iPhone, he has been waiting patiently. Waiting for her reaction.

They're just back from the main house–Alicia's parents' place–and are about to set up the bed in the sauna cottage, when Liam decides it's a good time to tell Alicia the news.

It's past eleven in the evening and Liam is tired, but he thinks the sooner he tells Alicia, the better. But his early start from London, the delay at Helsinki, and the choppy flight into Mariehamn have taken their toll on him. The compulsory meal Hilda cooked in Liam's honor included some kind of game in a creamy mushroom sauce and copious amounts of red wine, all which now rests heavily in his stomach. Luckily, they had decided before he arrived that they wouldn't insist on a sauna. Apparently, they would light one tomorrow. He calculates that if he'd been forced to endure an evening in a hot room, silently sweating with Uffe, his father-in-law, who speaks no English, his first evening on the islands would have stretched well past midnight.

'There'll be plenty of opportunity to have one before you go back to London,' Alicia had said with a wink as they sat in her old Volvo on their way from the airport to Sjoland. She knew how much Liam hated the sauna bathing ritual, and only suffered it because he didn't wish to offend Uffe or Hilda.

Alicia had been in a good mood when she picked him up. When they first set eyes on each other, she'd even replied to his kiss with enthusiasm, abandoning her mouth to his lips for much longer than she usually did. It gave Liam hope that she had finally come round to committing fully to their relationship.

Liam was further encouraged by the news that he was to sleep with Alicia in the sauna cottage. This was the first time since their brief separation last summer that he had not been banished to the attic room of the main house.

'Frida and little Anne Sofie are coming over for the holidays and I promised she could stay in the main house. It's much warmer and better with the baby. So you'll have to camp out in the sauna cottage with me.' Alicia grinned at Liam and her eyes had the playfulness they had before.

Before Liam ruined her life.

But he believed he was in the process of making good his mistakes, so he smiled back at her and placed his hand tentatively across the gearshift and onto her thigh. She didn't resist and let his hand rest there until she turned into the roundabout, which took them to Sjoland.

'I did it for you!' Liam now says. He doesn't understand her reaction. 'I thought that when you know the truth, you will see more clearly.'

The phone flew toward Liam at such speed that he barely managed to duck in time.

Alicia is staring at the man that she thought she knew. Liam is standing in front of her, holding the telephone she threw at him. It landed on the floor with a loud crack. She can see it has a deep slash across the screen. As if she cares! She's trying to understand how and why Liam has–against her clearly expressed objections–obtained a DNA test of little Anne Sofie.

'How?' Alicia now says.

Liam looks up from his phone and appears baffled for a moment, then his face brightens and he says, 'I know someone who runs a company doing these kinds of tests. It's the best one there is, so I am absolutely certain that these are correct. I can get you to talk to Steve.'

'I mean how did you get a sample from little Anne Sofie?' Alicia is trying to control her voice but her words come out almost as a growl.

'Oh, I took a strand from her hair. It didn't hurt her. She's got such a mop. And as you know, we have Stefan's.'

'You used the locks I kept from his hair?'

Liam looks at his hands. 'I had no choice.'

There's a silence. Alicia doesn't know what to say. Anger surges up, and she tries to concentrate on her breathing to try to calm down. She glances at the sofa bed, which they were about to open up. To think she had been considering sleeping with Liam tonight! She made the decision that day while making Christmas preparations with her mother. The way Patrick had ignited her desire might simply be because she missed intimacy, she'd reasoned; perhaps she will react in the same way with her husband? But now, she can't even imagine touching Liam.

There are so many things rushing through her mind. The violation of poor little Anne Sofie. When did Liam pull a hair out of her head? Did the baby notice? Cry? Oh, Alicia is so angry she has to hold herself to stop her from lashing out at Liam. And then there is the envelope of Stefan's hair that she had kept in the drawer of her dressing table in the bedroom in London. When she was there in the fall, she'd considered taking it with her, but she thought it belonged at home. Stefan's home. If they came to sell the house, she would then decide what to do with it. But for Liam to help himself and send her little boy's blond curls to some laboratory. It was just inconceivable!

'I know you're fond of both Frida and Anne Sofie.'

'Fond!' Alicia shouts.

Liam puts up his hands. One is holding the phone. Alicia notices that the screen is broken in two, but that the light is still on. She has to fight the temptation to snatch the device out of his hand and jump on it with both feet. But what would that achieve?

'Please, let me explain?' Liam says. 'Why don't we sit down?' he adds, trying to take hold of Alicia's arm and guide her to the sofa bed. But Alicia turns her body away and sits in one of the chairs set opposite the coffee table instead.

Suddenly Alicia thinks of her mother. With yesterday's revelations about the Russian loan shark, which haven't quite sunk in yet, this would just be too much for her mother to bear. Or would it? Last summer, when Alicia found out about Frida's pregnancy and the baby's paternity, Hilda hadn't exactly been convinced by it all. She didn't have to say it, but Alicia knows Hilda would rather not be related to Frida's late mother, Sirpa Anttila. She was only a waitress, after all.

Alicia puts her head in her hands. The snobbery on this island!

Liam is looking out of the darkened window.

Alicia follows his gaze. It's pitch-black beyond the snow bank outside the window and the icy sea farther on. In the summer, it never gets dark but in the winter it never seems to get fully light, even with fresh snow on the ground.

'Go on,' Alicia says. She can't take in the news Liam has told her, nor can she understand why he would do such a thing. She can't believe that after everything that has happened he is trying to take away the thing that is most precious to her.

'You know I always had my doubts about the baby,' Liam says.

Alicia wants to scream that 'the baby' he's talking about is the most important human being in her life, but through enormous effort, she manages to keep her mouth shut. So she nods instead, and lets Liam carry on.

'So last time I was here, I noticed the little nail scissors Frida has in her changing bag and when you two left me alone with Anne Sofie, I simply cut a tiny bit of hair from her head. Honestly, she didn't feel a thing.'

'When did you get the results?' Alicia asks. Again she manages to keep her voice level, even though she wants to get up and shout in Liam's ear. And pound her fists into his chest.

'About a week ago. I didn't want to tell you over the phone.'

There is a silence. Alicia wonders how she can tell Liam the extent of the devastation he has caused with his actions, how violated she feels on behalf of herself and little Anne Sofie. And Frida.

'I'd throw you out but I know you won't be able to get a cab into Mariehamn at this hour. Not in mid-winter. But tomorrow, you're on your own,' Alicia says. She gets up and yanks at the sofa bed.

With her back to Liam, she pulls open the chest of drawers where she keeps her bedding. 'The chair is yours,' she adds and throws a woolen blanket toward him.

TWENTY-NINE

Alicia doesn't fall sleep until the early hours. She keeps looking over at Liam, who is slumped in the chair, with his head resting backward uncomfortably. Still, he is fast asleep, gently snoring. Does the man have any feelings at all? Does he not know that her world has fallen apart. Again? And if he knows, which surely he must by now, how can he sleep so soundly?

She can't believe that the wonderful, now fully smiling, gurgling baby girl that she fell in love with the first time she held her, isn't related to her by blood. Nor to Stefan. She looks so much like him, with her combination of blonde curls and blue eyes. Of course, there's some of Frida in her too, particularly in the curve of her chin, but Alicia can't believe she would have imagined all the similarities to Stefan.

Anne Sofie has his long limbs and body. Even as a baby her son looked like the thin, gangly teenager he so soon became. Just like Stefan, Anne Sofie didn't have any of the rolls of fat most babies have in their thighs and arms. Instead, she has lean arms and strong legs, which she kicks, trying to grab them at every opportunity.

Alicia cannot help a smile forming on her lips and she reaches out to her phone to look at the most recent pictures of the baby. She is so beautiful, with a mischievous smile and a glint in her eyes, as if she knows she's got everyone wrapped around her little finger.

Everyone apart from Liam, it seems.

Toward the early hours of the morning, after a night mainly spent trying to sleep, and an awful dream in which Liam took Anne Sofie to the police station and told Ebba, the Chief of Police, that she was an imposter, Alicia realizes something. It doesn't matter to her if Anne Sofie really is Stefan's daughter or not.

She knows the test is probably right, and that Frida has unwittingly (or on purpose) misled her, and that she will have to ask her about it at some point in the future. But for now, Alicia *feels* like Anne Sofie's grandmother, so that is what she will be. With the death of Frida's mother, the poor little mite has no one else, so why shouldn't she help out? Frida obviously also believes that Stefan is the father, so what harm can there be in forgetting about the stupid test and carrying on as before?

If it's finally over with Liam, she can examine her feelings toward Patrick. From the kiss she knows her body still hankers after his touch. But is she one of those women (like Brit, she cannot help but think) who jump from man to man with speed and without so much as a glance back?

In the small hours, as she listens to Liam's snoring (how can the man sleep?), she aches for Patrick. She hasn't seen or heard from him since he kissed her and asked her to move to Stockholm with him. She has a great temptation to send him a message, but she manages to stop herself. What would Patrick think of a message in the middle of the night? It's like being a teenager again, sending covert declarations of love to each other. Besides, he knows Liam is back on the islands, so he'd know she was thinking of him while she is with her husband. Alicia cannot let him know that.

Suddenly the desire to leave all of this—the DNA test, her marriage, Hilda and Uffe and their problems with the Russian—is too great. Could she do it?

Alicia decides she can't think about that now, not when she needs to arrange the first family Christmas on the islands for years. She resolves to face it all in the New Year with a clear head.

THIRTY

The text from Frida takes Alicia by surprise. It's short and just says, *'Can you come and see us this lunchtime?'*

'Of course! Just before 12 noon?' Alicia adds three heart emojis to her reply. It's unusual for Frida to contact her, it's normally her who gets in touch first. Asking how the baby is doing, and if Frida needs any help. Often the reply is a 'No,' so Alicia has to invent reasons to visit mother and baby.

Alicia has got used to Frida's rather abrupt demeanor and she totally understands that having anyone, let alone your 'mother-in-law' around when the baby is small can be a little overwhelming. Besides, she has just lost her mother, which must be just dreadful for her.

Yet when Alicia thinks back to when Stefan was newborn and a toddler, she would have done almost anything to have an older woman around. Liam's parents had died when he was at university, and Hilda could only stay with her a week or two at a time. How she had longed to be able to call someone at short notice, or to ask someone to babysit, so she could have an hour or so of uninterrupted sleep. But, Alicia muses, baby Anne Sofie is very good at sleeping. Already at nearly four months, she needs just one feed at night and has two (regular) good naps during the day. Oh, what Alicia would have given for that! Stefan didn't like to sleep at night, during the day, or ever, really. For at least six months after his birth, Alicia went about the house in a sleepless trance, rocking the crying Stefan, who had suffered from terrible colic, night and day. Liam had started at a new hospital and had crazy hours.

Alicia sits herself down at her desk in the newspaper office and looks at the time on her mobile. She has two hours to write an article about holiday opening hours on the islands. She's looked at last year's piece, which Harri, the editor attached to his email telling her to *Just copy & paste.'* There has been absolutely no 'real' news on the islands for days now. Everyone is busy getting ready for Christmas. Most of the Christmas parties, which provided some fodder with their disturbances and complaints from residents in the center of town, are over and people are just gathering with their families and loved ones to eat gingerbread biscuits and drink mulled wine while preparing for the Christmas Eve feast.

She should really be trying to find out more about Dudnikov, but she's found nothing at all so far. A virtual brick wall seems to surround the man.

She sighs, perhaps this paper and this town are too provincial for her?

Whereas Stockholm …

After what Liam has done, she cannot see herself ever being able to forgive him. She left him at the house with Hilda that morning. He offered to come with her into town, but Alicia just gave him a short 'No,' and kissed her mother goodbye. Hilda was standing at the sink with her back to both of them, so Alicia hopes she didn't notice the chilly atmosphere between them.

'Let's all have lunch in town!' Hilda said, just as Alicia was at the door, thinking she'd escaped.

Alicia muttered something about work, and it being the last day before the holidays, but Hilda ignored her and arranged to meet in town at noon.

Alicia quickly gets her phone out and sends Liam a message.'Can't come to lunch, work thing.' She sends a similar but a little more wordy message to Hilda.

After she's posted the article on shopping hours to the intranet for the editor to approve and publish, Alicia goes into the little kitchen in the newspaper office and pours herself some coffee. Someone has brought in homemade Christmas stars, traditional flaky pastries shaped like stars with prune filling in the middle. Alicia picks one up, and just as she's biting into it, Kim comes into the kitchen.

Alicia nods to the lad, who doesn't blush as he usually does, but smiles.

'Are they good? My mom made them.'

'Very,' Alicia replies. She places the half-eaten tart on a piece of kitchen paper and starts to head past Kim out of the door.

'Hmm, I hope you don't mind, but I noticed you were looking for information about a person called Alexander Dudnikov?'

Alicia regards the young intern, who is wearing a freshly pressed blue shirt and neat dark jeans.

'Yeah, why?'

'If you want, I think I can help you with that.'

Frida opens the door to her ground-floor apartment. Alicia notices that the living room is in turmoil, there is a packet of diapers open on the floor, next to wet wipes and a tube of cream. A pile of baby clothes sits in one corner of the room and as she glances into the kitchen, Alicia sees a stack of dirty dishes in and around the sink.

She gives Frida a hug, moves a pair of torn jeans and a hoodie from the sofa, and sits down.

'Baby asleep?' she asks when Frida, clearing a space for herself on an armchair opposite, sits down and pulls her bare feet under her legs. She's wearing black leggings and a long black and red checked shirt. Her hair has grown a little, and is no longer the color of a rainbow, but pale brown. Her toenails are bright blue, though, so the girl hasn't lost all of her quirkiness through motherhood. Looking at Frida's still cropped head, Alicia absentmindedly thinks again that Anne Sofie must have got her blonde locks from Stefan.

And then she remembers.

Stefan is not the baby's father and I am not the grandmother.

Frida nods. She hesitates for a moment, and then says, 'I've read my mother's will.'

'Really?' Alicia can't quite understand how Sirpa Anttila, a waitress, would have needed to write a will. She was under the impression that her mother's—and now

144

Frida's—small apartment was a rental and that she had no property, or savings. Or perhaps she did?

'Yeah, and it seems I am now quite rich.'

Alicia doesn't say anything. After a while she's aware that her mouth is open, and has been for some time. She closes it and sees that Frida is smirking.

'She left me just under a million Euros and this apartment, so you don't have to worry about me anymore. There's no need for you and Liam to help me so much.'

'How?'

At Alicia's simple question, Frida appears a little discombobulated.

'It seems she had a benefactor.'

Alicia thinks for a moment.

'But you know we'll always want to make sure you're OK. It's not a question of money,' she says.

Frida gazes at her with an expression Alicia finds difficult to interpret. Has Liam spoken to her? Surely he wouldn't dare?

'In any case, I thought you'd like to know,' Frida says finally.

THIRTY-ONE

Hilda is looking through her various Christmas lists in the kitchen. She has so much to do. She has to cook the vegetable bakes and check on the various marinated herring dishes she's been making in the week leading up to the holidays, as well as the gravlax that Alicia prepared. And she has to remind her daughter to fetch the ham. It needs to go in the oven tonight, so that it's ready for tomorrow.

Liam is already here and she has no idea what to do with him. Alicia has gone off to work, and left the poor man alone. There was a definite atmosphere between the two earlier that morning, so even if they shared the sauna cottage last night, Hilda very much doubts that they slept together. How can a married couple live thousands of miles away from each other and still have a sex life? Besides, she's seen how Alicia acts when she talks about Patrick. And now he's divorced from Mia Eriksson, leaving the coast clear for another woman. She's tried to find out from Uffe what the gossip about the Eriksson girl is, but he says they're all tight-lipped about it. It's at times like these that Hilda regrets not having the boutique. Even though there weren't that many customers, the old village gossips would pop in and update her on what was happening on the islands. Now she's completely in the dark. Perhaps she should take Uffe's advice and join the local women's club, the Lionesses? A suggestion Hilda laughed at when Uffe made it.

'Me, a member of that knitting circle? Please!' she'd said, and that was the end of that conversation.

As she enters the lounge to ask if the men want another cup of coffee, she sees her husband is fast asleep in an armchair. His mouth is open and he's snoring gently, his gray mustache quivering slightly at each breath. Hilda stands above Uffe for a moment. She wonders what secrets he is withholding from her. What does he know about Dudnikov that he hasn't told her?

Although it had been a frightening incident, the run-in with the Russian provided her with some excitement.

Forget about that terrible man!

No, Hilda needs to concentrate on the family Christmas. They will want for nothing. She goes over to the other chair, on the opposite side of the lounge, where Liam is reading on his iPad.

'More coffee?'

Her son-in-law smiles at her but shakes his head.

So Hilda goes back to her lists, which she has carried with her everywhere since they returned from Spain. Suddenly she sees something on it and remembers that she needs to look into the linen. Does she have enough Christmas napkins? And are the matching tablecloths that she will need for Liam's week-long visit all pressed and spotless? How can she have forgotten such an important detail!

Hilda hurries to the far end of the lounge, where she keeps the linen in an old cabinet. It's not until she's by the large window overlooking the fields that she notices the change in weather. It's sunny, the rays shining down to the whitened ground. The view is breathtaking.

How wonderful, it's going to be a special Christmas!

THIRTY-TWO

While she's been with Frida, Alicia has received several messages from Hilda and Liam. She sees Liam has asked why they can't meet for lunch, but hasn't sent anything after the first text. Her mother, on the other hand, has reminded her to pick up the ham, more dill and butter, adding Christmas wrapping paper in a second message and festive name tags in a third. Alicia doesn't understand why she hasn't driven into town herself until she listens to a voicemail from Hilda.

'Look, can you call? We can't get hold of you anywhere. Harri at the newspaper says you left just after noon and he hasn't heard from you since!' There's a pause and then, Hilda says in a lower voice, 'I'm here with Liam. I think it would be rude to leave him alone, and he hasn't wanted to do anything since you blew us off at lunchtime. Ring as soon as you get this!'

Alicia glances at her watch: it's just gone half past two. Her mother's voice sounded as if she has been away for weeks rather than a few hours. She sighs and dials Hilda's number.

'There you are! I was getting really worried.'

Alicia cuts her mother short, 'I need to go back to work, but I'll pop over to the store on my way home. It's open late tonight, isn't it? I'm not sure if I can get away early today.'

'Oh,' Hilda says. 'What's going on? Where have you been? There can't be any big news stories this close to Christmas!'

Alicia laughs out loud. 'Yes, Mother, the world shuts down for the Christian festivities although only a third of its population is Christian.'

'Don't be clever with me. And don't change the subject!' Hilda tuts. And again, lowering her voice, she says, 'Your husband is here. He's been waiting all day for you.'

'Well, he knows I work so he'll just have to wait a little longer. Take him shopping!' Alicia says, hoping that her mother will take the bait.

'You better talk to him,' she says instead, and without hearing Alicia's protests, she hands the phone to Liam.

After a few moments, during which there's a stilted conversation between her husband and mother, she hears Liam's voice.

'Alicia?'

'Look, I'm not going to be back until late tonight, so you might as well go shopping with Hilda.'

'Erm, I,' Liam starts, but Alicia interrupts him.

'I've got to go.' She disconnects the line and leans

back on her chair. She looks up and sees Kim's eyes upon her.

'Sorry I didn't have time to talk to you before. I needed to be somewhere. You said you could help me track down Dudnikov?'

Kim blushes again, but says in a confident voice, 'It's not really the done thing, but I can access Stockholm police files. I came across someone of the same name, Alexander Dudnikov, right?'

Alicia nods. She's thinking about how illegal all of this is, but decides it's probably OK for now. Until she acts upon this information, nothing will have been unlawful, will it?

Kim starts to speak quickly now.

'I've been doing some private research into Eastern European crime on Åland and I came across the guy. Then I saw that a search for him had already been made from this office and that it was you.'

Alicia sits down beside Kim. They are the only two reporters in the room, apart from the editor, who's sitting at his desk in his fishbowl office. Alicia nodded a hello to him when she entered the office. Luckily Harri isn't the talkative sort, so he didn't bother to pick her up about Hilda's earlier call. It wasn't the first time her mother rang her at work. She must speak to her about it. Alicia is nearly forty and not a child anymore!

'Is there a mugshot?'

Kim smiles, and, for the first time, seems relaxed talking to her.

'Ta-da!' He flicks the mouse and an image of the man

that nearly ran into her a couple of days ago in Föglö fills the screen.

'That's him.'

'He's got a record in Stockholm and is on the run as we speak. Convicted for extortion, with suspicions of money laundering and people trafficking, although they didn't have enough evidence to get him on those two more serious charges.'

'And he's here in Åland, lording over everyone!' Alicia exclaims.

'What do you mean? Have you got some evidence of his activities here?' Kim's face is turned toward Alicia, with an eager expression in his eyes.

Her instincts about Kim were correct, Alicia thinks briefly. He's going to make a brilliant reporter.

'Yes, but nothing concrete. There's also,' she hesitates for a moment, but decides that she can trust this young man.

'He may have been using banks here to launder funds.'

'Really! Can you prove it?'

'No,' Alicia says and adds, 'This is between you and me.'

Kim nods.

'Besides, we can't very well report things that we found illegally by hacking into another country's police files without having any other proof, can we?' Alicia adds, knowing full well that there are ways in which that can be done. By simply quoting 'unknown sources,' for example. Although it would be risky, all the same. Her words seem to have the desired effect and Kim returns to his desk.

Alicia ponders what she should do. It's tempting to go to Harri this minute with all the information, and ask if she can write a long piece on Dudnikov. But wouldn't that just make him more determined to scare Hilda and Uffe even more? He could do anything, Alicia is convinced of that. Goodness knows what kind of organization he is part of, or even heads. He can't be running this scam on his own, she's sure of it.

THIRTY-THREE

I t wasn't until they were disembarking that afternoon that Brit sees Jukka again. It was a busy morning crossing from Helsinki, with half of the crew changing over. There were members of staff Brit hadn't yet met and she needed to speak with them. Luckily this was the last shift that Brit would do with Kerstin. The woman obviously didn't like her. Whether it was jealousy over her being Kerstin's boss, Brit didn't know, but every time she saw her, the older woman either didn't speak to her or visibly sneered at her comments. At one point, when the lunch time rush in the buffet restaurant was at its worst, and Brit had taken the decision to let the next lot of passengers wait for fifteen minutes before being seated, Kerstin actually snorted. Brit gave her a stern look, but decided that since they wouldn't be working together anymore, she'd let it pass.

Light snow fell as they pulled away from Helsinki Harbor, only an hour and a half after they'd docked. While supervising the second breakfast sitting for the freshly arrived passengers, Brit caught a glimpse of the view through the vast windows. The city, dominated by the Cathedral with its large green dome surrounded by smaller domes and neoclassical columns, looked spectacular. It wasn't yet fully light, but the Cathedral clock shone through the snowflakes, as did the round old-fashioned streetlights outside the Presidential Palace and Town Hall by the water's edge. The ice and snow in the harbor had been broken up by the ferry traffic from the larger ships like *Sabrina* and the smaller boats taking passengers to the Helsinki archipelago. The frozen sea had a luminous bluish color. It moved in slow motion, like a vast bath overfilled with bath salts.

Suddenly, as she steps out of the terminal building in Mariehamn, Brit feels dog tired. She glances toward her bike standing under a shelter, and sees that this hasn't protected it from sidewinds. There is a thick layer of snow on top of the seat. Brit swears under her breath as she undoes the frozen lock on the front wheel.

'Hello!'

Brit turns around abruptly, sending the tiny key into the air.

'Damn!' she exclaims. She's lost the key in the thick layer of snow. She glances toward the parking lot behind her. Jukka is standing by his car, one leg inside, shouting something to her, but his words are caught in the wind.

'What?'

Even before Brit can begin to start looking for the key, he's next to her.

'Come on, I'll drive you home.'

'I lost the key. It's somewhere on the ground,' She points to the thick bank of snow. It'll be impossible to find anything underneath it. Brit swears under her breath once again.

'Listen, you can come and get it when the weather improves?'

The man's eyes look sincere, but Brit has had enough of his toing and froing. Besides, all she wants is a warm shower, a glass of wine, something to eat, and a romcom on TV.

'No, it's OK,' she says, dropping to her knees to try to find the key.

But Jukka stops her before she hits the ground. He takes her arm. 'Look, it's just a lift!'

Brit glances down at the snow. There's absolutely no sign of anything on the brilliant white surface.

She looks up at Jukka's eyes. They are friendly and the beginnings of a smile is dancing on his lips. She realizes that she's being stupidly stubborn.

Damn you.

Brit gives in. She lets herself be led by one arm to Jukka's car. Inside she revels in its warmth. The seats are heated, and a blast of warm air is coming from the vents either side of the panel in front of her. She didn't realize how cold she was.

'Sorry,' she says to Jukka, who is maneuvering the car out of the parking lot and into the main road leading to the center of Mariehamn.

'I really didn't want to leave the bike behind.'

Brit doesn't know what to say next.

And since I don't know what you want from me, I don't want to spend more time with you.

'No worries,' Jukka says and adds, 'Where can I take you?'

'Oh, the apartment is in the old fishing port.'

Jukka whistles, 'Not bad.'

They are soon at the crossroads at Ålandsvägen where Jukka takes a right. While he drives, Brit considers his profile for a moment. He has a strong nose, and a straight, firm jaw.

As they are making their way south, Brit says, 'I hope I'm not taking you too much out of your way?'

Jukka turns briefly to gaze at Brit, and again that look of pleasure is hovering on his face.

'It doesn't matter. I couldn't leave a colleague out in this weather.'

A colleague.

Brit doesn't reply to this. Instead she turns her face toward the window. The landscape looks beautiful. The low-slung wooden villas in this part of the city are decorated for the season. Some have paper lanterns in the shape of stars shining out of the windows, and small Christmas trees strung with fairy lights twinkle in the front gardens. Soon they are in a wooded area, and then Brit can see the old block of apartments on her left. She remembers that another schoolfriend lived in one of the blocks, but she cannot for the life of her remember her name now.

Brit is stirred from her thoughts by a coughing sound.

'It's here?' he says as they near the turning to the old fishing port.

'Yes.'

Brit directs him to her block and after thanking him for the ride, she goes to open the door on her side. But before she can do that, Jukka stops her by placing a hand on her arm.

'Can I send you a message later?'

THIRTY-FOUR

Jukka drives home through the snowy landscape. Apart from a few years in Gothenburg after he finished his Sea Captain's Degree at Chalmers University, he has never lived anywhere else but on the islands. But rarely has the scenery appeared so stunning to him. As he drives along the East Harbor and sees the lights on a small strip of land that juts out of the largest landmass in Åland, across the water, he thinks what a lucky man he is. The dimness of the early afternoon adds an unreal quality to the scenery in front of him. Although he is tired, he decides he'll stay up with a cup of coffee when he gets home, simply to appreciate the view from his apartment in Solberg.

He bought the place, which has uninterrupted views over Slemmern toward the city, after his divorce from Leila was completed two years ago. He doesn't want to think about his ex, or the acrimonious divorce, which has left him estranged not only from his wife of over fifteen years but also from his teenage daughter, Silja. Jukka sighs and parks his car in the heated carport under the block of six apartments. He has the uppermost floor, which he paid over the odds for just to get the view. He still finds it funny that the locals call this admittedly expensive development consisting of terraced, semi-detached and detached villas, plus a handful of small luxury blocks of apartments, Gräddhyllan-Cream Shelf. But he's more than happy to be considered entitled: he's worked hard for what he's achieved. Jukka didn't have a rich family to rely on when he was growing up. His father was a seafaring man like himself, but unlike Jukka, he was never at home. He worked on freight vessels all over the world, wherever he could get onto the crew, and occasionally, perhaps for Christmas and Easter, he'd honor his family with his presence.

Which wasn't wanted.

Jukka's father, Ville Markusson was an alcoholic, and a violent one at that. Jukka, as the only child, soon learned to duck and hide while his old man was at home. His poor mother bore the brunt of his father's alcohol-induced mirth. When Jukka was old enough to speak his mind, he begged his mother, Pirkko, to leave him.

'But what are we going to do for money?'

Pirkko, who had married Jukka's father when they'd met in Turku, worked as a cleaner for the offices in town and was always scrimping and saving. Her Swedish wasn't very good. She'd never learned it properly. She'd left school at sixteen and started to work on the Stockholm ferries. By eighteen, she was pregnant with Jukka and Ville did the honorable thing and married her, even though he'd only spent a handful of nights with her. He brought his new bride home to Åland and promptly went away to sea, leaving her alone in a council property.

The only good that came out of his father was the monthly payment he deposited into Pirkko's bank account. When the payments suddenly stopped, when Jukka was at university in Gothenburg, he received a panicked call from his mother. Before he had time to travel home (with an emergency grant from the student's union), a letter had arrived telling Pirkko that her husband had died following an accident in the ship's machine room.

Jukka was sure his mother never loved the violent man —she'd spent her life fearing his returns to the family home—but after his small funeral, it took only six months for Pirkko to perish too. Never more than skin and bones, she seemed to become tired of living.

Jukka shakes his head, and makes himself a coffee. He needs to halt these dark thoughts now. But he can't stop thinking about his mother's funeral, which was an even smaller affair than Ville's, if that is possible. Jukka, who was on the largest grant possible from the education panel in the islands, as well as a scholarship from the prestigious university he was attending, Chalmers, had managed to pay for the casket and the service out of the savings he'd put aside when he'd worked as a waiter in a posh restaurant in Gothenburg. His aunt, Sirpa's only sister had traveled from Turku and had organized some food and drinks to be served in the small apartment in Jomala. Looking at the coffin being lowered into the ground, Jukka had promised himself that he would never be poor, and that he would make better use of his life than either his mother or father had.

So this is it.

A better life.

Jukka leans back in his Artek designer chair that he bought five years ago when the divorce from Leila was absolute. It was the first piece of furniture he'd got for his new apartment after they'd sold the large family house.

He decided to keep the style of the new place simple with natural tones. All the furniture was black, including the woven leather seat he was reclining in. The floors were pale wood as was his kitchen table (also from Artek), which sat six people. Not that he'd ever hosted such a large dinner party.

There were Venetian blinds on all the large windows, so he just needed thin drapes either end, which didn't even have to meet in the middle. That's what the woman in the shop in Mariehamn told him when he went in to inquire about window coverings. It was the fashion nowadays, she'd told him. Jukka decided on a pale gray fabric and the woman organized the rest, even coming over to fit them. She stood in front of the wide window in the living room, where he was now sitting, admiring the view.

'I can now see why they charge so much for these houses,' she said and turned to Jukka. He just shrugged. With his wife and daughter out of the picture, there was no one making demands on his salary, although he did pay a sum into his daughter's account every month.

·   ·   ·

The coffee on the small table next to his chair has gone cold and it's grown dark. The view out of Jukka's window now resembles something out of a picture book or a travel website. The water in front of him is snow covered ice, the color of the palest of blues. In front of him, the city of Mariehamn opens up. He can see the lights of the small red wooden buildings, their roofs covered in thick virgin snow, straight to the right, and beyond that the flickering lights of the city itself. He can just make out St George Church spire in the distance. He remembers how, when young, and so in love, he and Leila tied the knot there. The church had seemed too large for the two families, especially as Jukka only had his aunt in attendance, but he insisted.

'You always had ideas above your station.'

Leila spat the words out during a heated row toward the end of the marriage. He can't even remember what they were arguing about now. Leila was a good wife and a mother, but in the end he just grew apart from her. It was just as well she found out about Sia. Otherwise he might still be living a double life, which wasn't healthy for anyone.

THIRTY-FIVE

'*How about a drink tonight. Meet me at Arkipelag bar 6pm?*'

Brit stares at the message on her phone. She'd just stopped for a cappuccino in town when the cold eventually got to her, freezing her right to the bone. She'd been dragging herself through the shops all after-noon in search of last minute presents for Alicia's family. She has no idea what Hilda would like, let alone Uffe or Liam. In the end she opts for an Amaryllis just in bud, potted into a glass vase for Alicia's mother, and a bottle of cognac each for Uffe and Liam. She bought three bottles from the ferry, together with a case of champagne, some of which she will take over on Christmas Eve.

It's so kind of Hilda to invite her and her father over to the house in Sjoland. They have even offered to put them up for the night, even though Rolf had insisted they should drive home.

'The last ferry to Föglö goes at 7pm, and we're prob-ably not going to sit down to eat before six!' Brit told her father over the phone, so eventually he agreed to the arrangement.

Brit glances at the text again. Earlier that day she was annoyed with the man, but now she has calmed down. She's more of less done with her shopping. She's already got Alicia's present from the ferry's tax-free shop, which to her amazement was well stocked with the latest brands. She's sure Alicia will appreciate the soft fur-lined leather gloves. Rubbing her hands together, Brit regrets that she didn't get a pair for herself too. Perhaps she will next time she's on duty. She got something for Mia too (an expensive cashmere and silk scarf, also from the ferry's shop), although she's apparently not going to be on the islands for Christmas. Mia sent her a message in the week, with an image of herself and the two girls on skis. The whole Eriksson family is spending the holidays in their mountain lodge in the Swedish ski resort of Åre.

Brit lets her mind wander while she decides what to do about Jukka. In any case, he can wait for a reply. Instead of messaging Jukka, Brit finds Alicia's number in her phone and presses 'ring.'

The call goes straight to voice mail. She tries again after a few minutes, but no luck. She must be working, Brit thinks and glances down at her outfit. She's wearing a pair of tight black jeans and a loose jumper with a see-through v-section at the front, which rather attractively shows off her cleavage, and has her lace-up boots on. Although low-heeled, they are quite sexy in a biker-girl kind of way.

This'll do.

Brit taps a message onto her phone.

'Sorry can't tonight, but in town now. Meet me at A in 15?'

Jukka spots Brit immediately in the darkened bar. She's sipping a glass of champagne (what else?) and chatting animatedly with the barman, who's very tall and handsome and at least ten years younger than Brit.

And him.

He stalls for time while he takes in her body. Tight jeans, black boots and a jumper that somehow, although loose, shows off her skin at the back. When he walks toward her, and places his hand proprietarily around her waist, he can see the top is partly sheer at the back and the front.

She is gorgeous, what are you waiting for?

'Hello,' he says and brushes her on the cheek with his lips, as close to her red-painted mouth as he can without actually kissing her.

'Hi,' Brit says. She gazes at him, but doesn't say anything else.

Jukka tears his eyes away from her and orders a beer. When the dark, curly-haired barman hands Jukka the drink, he nods to a sofa farther into the bar and asks Brit if she'd like to move to sit somewhere more comfortable.

The place is heaving with party-goers even this early in the afternoon, but then it's nearly Christmas. There's seasonal music playing and large, red, gold and silver baubles hanging from the ceiling.

'So,' he utters, struggling to know what to say. Brit is so good-looking that suddenly he wonders if she's above his league. Her cheeks are a little flushed and the red lipstick is really flattering, as is her outfit. Her legs seem to go on forever in those jeans. His glance moves down to her boots. What he'd give to unlace them later.

'So,' she replies, and gives a small laugh. 'Have you seen something you like?'

Brit stretches a hand toward the low table between them and grabs her glass. She leans back again and takes a sip of her champagne.

'I'm sorry. I'm rather stunned at how beautiful you are looking tonight.'

Now Brit laughs out loud.

'Isn't that a song?'

Jukka laughs with her. 'Might be. Still true.'

This is good, I'm making her laugh.

Leaning in to him, revealing even more of her delicious cleavage, and wearing a coquettish expression, Brit says, 'What is it you want, Captain Markusson?'

'I want to take you to bed.'

THIRTY-SIX

Ebba Torstensson sits with her hands crossed over the almost empty desk. It's immaculately tidy in the police chief's office. No piles of case papers, no images of criminals, or even pictures of family. Alicia regards her old schoolfriend. Tall, slim, and always straight-talking to the point of being rude, Ebba was always a bit of a loner at school. Alicia only really got to know her better the previous summer, even though they'd studied at Uppsala University outside Stockholm at the same time. But Alicia was on a journalism course, while Ebba had her head deep in thick volumes of criminology. Alicia would sometimes spot her in the university library, and nod a greeting, but she doesn't remember ever going for a drink with her.

In the summer, however, when Alicia, together with Patrick, investigated the death of Daniel, the Romanian boy, who turned out to be a friend of both her late son Stefan as well as Frida, Alicia relied on her police friend for information about the investigation. In the end, it turned out to be a tragic accident. But Ebba and Alicia became friends, or at least professionally connected. Alicia now wonders if the police chief has any close friends at all.

'So let me get this right. You want me to ask for information from the Swedish police on a known–wanted–Russian criminal?'

'Yes, I'd do it myself but I think coming from you, it would be better.'

'And you think he is here, in Åland?'

'Yes.' Alicia bends her head and looks at her hands. She's sitting on the other side of the immaculate desk. She knows what's coming next.

'And exactly how do you know about all this?'

Alicia sighs and lifts her eyes toward Ebba.

'I can't reveal my sources.'

'How did I know you'd say that?' Ebba's inquisitive eyes are steadily gazing at Alicia.

'Look,' she says, leaning toward her old schoolfriend. 'Just think, if it is him, and you arrest him and hand him over to Stockholm, you'll be recognized for the capture both over there and here. Plus you would have stopped the criminal activities of a loan shark, money launderer and goodness knows what other illegal activities Dudnikov is engaged in.'

'Hmm.' Ebba looks unconvinced.

'I believe he has been laundering money through a person you and I know.'

This is Alicia's trump card, and she is rewarded by a look of interest in the police chief's eyes.

'A crime here, on the islands?'

'Plus extortion.'

'Wait here.' Ebba gets up and once again Alicia is surprised at the woman's height. She must be nearly two meters tall! The police chief walks past Alicia without saying another word and closes the door behind her.

Alicia is fidgeting. The heating in Ebba's office is on full blast and she is sweltering under her padded coat. It's already gone past 5:30pm and she still needs to get the ham from the supermarket. Ebba has been out of the room for fifteen minutes now, and there's no sign of her, so Alicia removes her coat and goes to stand by the window overlooking the parking lot of the police head-quarters. And there, she spots the police chief stepping into a car, together with two policemen. They drive off, sirens blaring.

What the hell?

Alicia swears under her breath. She picks up her coat from the back of the chair and darts down the stairs, but by the time the cold air hits her body, the police car is too far away for her to catch up with it. She can see its flick-ering lights and hear the siren in the dusk. It's driving at top speed out of the city on the main thoroughfare skim-ming the East Harbor.

Alicia sends a message to Ebba.

'What's going on?'

She stands outside, shivering in the late afternoon chill, then realizes she hasn't put her coat on. No message from the police chief, not that Alicia was expecting one. Again, she curses silently into the deserted parking lot in front of the police headquarters. This area is illuminated by bright streetlights and the few dark patches where parked cars have melted the snow make the space look like a huge checkerboard. Alicia decides to go back inside to see if anyone can tell her why and where Ebba took off, but naturally, as expected, the policeman at the front desk is more than tight-lipped about her schoolfriend's movements.

She's trying to decide what to do–go after Ebba in the hope she'll find the police car somewhere along the four roads that lead off the main intersection. Or go home via the supermarket? She's sure Hilda is having kittens by now, and Liam will be bored out of his skull in Sjoland.

That's when she gets a message from Frida.

'Ring me, I have some major news.'

Frida's phone rings for several minutes with no answer.

Alicia sits in her car. She decides to head off into the Kantarellen shop to pick up the ham and try Frida again when she's there. She ends a quick message to her mother, asking if there's anything else she needs to get. Alicia isn't looking forward to the inevitable Christmas rush in the shop, but she can't avoid it. She knows Hilda needs to cook the ham tonight for it to be ready in time for the festivities. Just as she's indicating left on the coastal road, she gets a message back from her mother.

'We've been to the shops with Liam and ham is already in the oven. We're waiting for you to have the champagne. Come home!'

Alicia has no desire to celebrate, but she mustn't let her mother know that. She thinks for a moment and decides to pen a reply, saying she has some last-minute

Christmas shopping to do. Turning left, she and heads back into town again. She might as well go and see Frida to hear what other news the girl has. Perhaps this time little Anne Sofie is awake and Alicia can have a cuddle with her. She's come to depend on the love she feels for the baby, and the baby's affection for her, and she's not about to give that up. Whatever the stupid DNA test shows—and her cruel husband thinks she should do—she's still, at least in name only, Anne Sofie's grandma.

THIRTY-SEVEN

When Frida opens the door to Alicia, she is filled with the delicious smells of Christmas baking. There's cinnamon, cloves, and the irresistible scent of butterscotch. Frida's got one hand inside a red Marimekko oven glove and with the other, she's gesturing Alicia to step in.

'I'm baking gingerbread cookies and making *knäck*!'

Hence the delicious smell of burnt sugar and butter, Alicia thinks. She can't remember when she last had the Swedish Christmas sweets, and follows Frida into her small kitchen. What greets her is something close to chaos, in the middle of which is the gurgling and smiling Anne Sofie. She's sitting in a bouncing chair on the kitchen table, surrounded by packets of flour, sugar and spices, and two trays of biscuits. There seems to be flour everywhere, including on Anna Sofie's red and white striped onesie.

'Hello, sweetheart!' Alicia says, letting the baby take

hold of her little finger. She's just learned to play with her feet, an activity that seems to keep her occupied for hours.

'Isn't she good?' Alicia says.

'Yeah, well, when she's like this. You should have heard her scream blue murder earlier when I deigned to change madam's nappy.' Frida comes over and kisses the baby's forehead, before returning to the stove, where she is stirring the butterscotch mixture.

'This burns easily, I saw on the Youtube video, so if she kicks off, can you pick her up? There's a bottle in the fridge that you can warm in the micro and give her if need be. I'm trying to get her weaned off these.' Frida glances down at her chest.

'Really, already? Isn't it better for the baby to have at least six months of breastmilk?'

Frida doesn't say anything, but Alicia can tell she's– once again–overstepped the boundaries of her grand-motherhood. She sighs.

Have I turned into an interfering mother-in-law now?

Alicia is fighting the urge to pick up the baby straight away, but she fears that might elicit more silent disap-proval from Frida, so instead she sits at the table and just gazes at the beautiful child. Her eyes are so clear blue and her hair so blonde, Alicia cannot believe she doesn't have Stefan's genes.

'You said you had some news?' she asks Frida. She's still talking to her back, while Bing Crosby is singing 'White Christmas' next door in the living room. A song very apt at the moment. Outside Frida's kitchen, there's a snowbank that's nearly halfway up the darkened window.

While all the time stirring the pan, Frida says, 'Yeah, I

found out that someone called Alexander Dudnikov is the guy making all those payments into my mom's account. So I guess he must be my father.'

'What?' Alicia cannot believe what she has just heard. 'Did you say, *Alexander Dudnikov?*'

Now Frida turns round, the wooden spoon in her hand covered in the thick, brown candy mixture. 'Yeah, why?'

'How did you find out!'

'Just a minute,' Frida says and turns off the electric plate under the *knäck* mixture. 'I think this is ready, so I can pour it out. Could you hand me that tray?'

Finally, when the butterscotch mixture is cooling on a tray covered with parchment paper, Frida sits at the kitchen table opposite Alicia. She begins to talk, her words being carefully observed by little Anne Sofie, who has grown still and quiet in the bouncy chair between them.

'I got to thinking that it's really unfair for me not to know who's paying me all this money, or has been supporting my mom and me all this time. And I thought it must be illegal to keep me in the dark. And that I must have some right to the information?

'So I went online, had a look at the laws and whatnot and decided to lay it on a bit thick with old Mr Karlsson. And, of course, he cracked and told me everything he knew. Or at least I think he did.' Frida looks up from the baby, whose fair hair she's been stroking.

'He's a bit of a slippery number, that one,' she adds.

'What do you know about this Dudnikov?' Alicia's heart is racing. She isn't sure if she should tell Frida what she knows of the Russian. How he was wanted by the Swedish police and how he'd been intimidating Hilda, and possibly Uffe, and how he tried to run both her parents and Alicia off the icy roads. And goodness knows what other illegal and horrible deeds he was responsible for. And that Ebba, the police chief, was at this minute perhaps arresting Dudnikov and putting him on the next available flight to Stockholm and prison. All because she, Alicia, had told Ebba all about the Russian.

Frida's father and little Anne Sofie's grandfather.

Frida gives Alicia a smile.

'I've known for a while that my father is a Russian. You know what the rumor mill is like on the islands?'

Alicia nods.

'So last year, when mom was taken into the home and I found out I was up the, you know, I decided to find out once and for all. He was going to be a grandad, you know? But there was just nothing. Nothing in mom's paperwork, nothing online. I tried to ask mom, but when she had one of her clear days, she clammed up. Then, on one of her really bad days, she called out to a 'Sasha.' She kept repeating the name over and over, and got quite agitated, so I had to summon the nurses, who would give her something to make her sleep. It was awful.' Frida pulls at her apron, which is covered in flour and blotches of the yellow-brown spices, and dabs the corners of her eyes.

'Of course, I knew that Sasha is a nickname for someone called Alexander, so I went online and looked for anyone with that name who lived–or had lived–in Åland. But again, I drew a blank. It was so weird. Of course, I didn't know about Mr Karlsson and his role in keeping it all from me. Why I wasn't allowed to meet my dad, I still don't know. Especially as he's obviously not short of a penny or two and has supported us all these years!'

Alicia listens intently to Frida. The background music changes to a Finnish Christmas hymn.

'But that's all going to change now.' Frida bends down to kiss Anne Sofie's cheek and continues, 'He's going to get to know this little one as well as me.'

Alicia is alarmed, 'What do you mean? Have you been in touch with him?'

Frida lifts her eyes. Alicia can see the girl's eyes flash dark.

'You haven't got a monopoly over us, you know.'

THIRTY-EIGHT

Alicia's head is spinning. After Frida's revelation about her father, little Anne Sofie started to fuss and Frida made it clear that Alicia wasn't helping the situation.

'She's probably got colic,' Alicia suggested. 'There's no such thing,' Frida replied, over the cries of the baby, who was refusing Frida's attempts to feed her a bottle.

Anne Sofie was displaying all the signs of distress associated with the common baby complaint, pulling her little legs up to her tummy and getting red in the face. But when Frida turned away from Alicia and went into the small living room, trying to rock the baby to calm her down, Alicia decided that it was best for her to leave the new mother to it.

'Call me if you need anything, won't you?' Alicia spoke to Frida's back and gave both mother and baby a quick hug.

Now sitting in her car on her way home–at last–Alicia cannot believe that horrible individual, Alexander

Dudnikov, is little Anne Sofie's grandfather. She, as well as Frida, had heard the rumors about Frida's mother's Russian lover, but she didn't take them seriously. When Hilda told her last summer, Alicia was convinced that the woman had got pregnant and then invented a Russian to brush over the fact that she most likely didn't know who the father was. It was quite common in such a small community to blame any kinds of passing travelers for sudden pregnancies. And everything else.

That's mean—I didn't even know Frida's mother!

While she's been working at the paper, Alicia hasn't come across many petty crime stories where the culprit isn't from Sweden, Finland, or occasionally Russia. A recent—although rare—street mugging on a dark night in Mariehamn city center was put down to a Finnish national who (conveniently in Alicia's mind) managed to get on the ferry back to Finland before being arrested and was never heard of again.

Not that she thinks Ebba isn't good at her job—on the contrary—she's very conscientious, but Alicia suspects the islanders rarely drop each other into difficulties. They protect each other, unless something really bad happens, that is.

Alicia drives through the darkened roads back to Sjoland, her mind working hard on what she should do next. She's just ratted on little Anne Sofie's grandfather to the police! Alicia takes a quick glance at her phone but there's nothing from Ebba. She parks her car on the side of the road and dials the number of the police headquarters, but this time the officer at reception is even more abrupt and impolite.

'There is nothing we can tell the press at this stage. We will notify you as soon as we have anything. Please don't call again. You are wasting police time.'

Listening to the empty line, Alicia ends the call and throws her phone onto the passenger seat. Then she sends another message to Ebba, but once again, by the time she's nearing the swing bridge into Sjoland, there's still no reply.

Perhaps she should contact her editor, Harri, but by now he'll be at his summer cottage in the far archipelago and will not want to be disturbed. She's been told that the editor takes a full two weeks off over Christmas.

Besides, this has nothing to do with the paper as such. Harri would only tell her to write up everything she knows about Dudnikov and publish it. Whether it would hurt her family or not.

Alicia decides to contact the one person she knows will help her. She parks on the side of the canal, where a stand sells ice cream in summer. She dials Patrick's number.

'Hello gorgeous,' he says and Alicia wonders if he's been drinking.

Then she decides to stop being so judgmental. It is the last working day before Christmas after all, and past six o'clock, so even by her stuck-up English drinking time rules, it wouldn't be a crime to be a bit tipsy tonight.

'Patrick, I need your help.'

THIRTY-NINE

For the second time that day, Brit is in Jukka's car, this time driving north, toward Sjoland.

'Where do you live?' Brit asks as she watches the landscape becoming more and more dreamlike. After leaving Mariehamn behind, the snow envelopes them on all sides. Vast pillows of white cover the fields and hang off the occasional rows of pine trees.

'Oh, Gräddhyllan, I believe the area is generally called.'

Brit laughs; this is the expression Swedes give to any expensive seats at a sports match or an exclusive area of housing. Not something in Åland.

'I've never heard of that.'

'Solberg isn't much better,' Jukka says. Brit can't see his face fully in the dim light of the car, but she can hear the smile in his voice. And Brit agrees, 'Sunny Mountain' doesn't exactly suit these craggy islands either.

But she changes her mind as soon she steps inside Jukka's third-floor apartment. The view is even more impressive than the one she enjoys from her apartment. The sun has long since set, so it can't be called 'sunny,' but she sees how this place can be called exclusive. In the distance, she sees Mariehamn open out in front of her. With the freshly fallen snow covering the rooftops and the twinkling lights from Christmas decorations and buildings, it looks like a picture postcard. Jukka's block is right at the top of the 'Sunny Mountain'–more of a hill–and has uninterrupted views of the city, the frozen sea, and some of the small islands outside Mariehamn.

'How do you get anything done?' Brit glances around and realizes that Jukka is standing right behind her.

Instead of replying, he takes hold of her waist and bends down to kiss her neck. The touch of his lips against her skin sends a signal down Brit's spine and she lets out an involuntary sigh.

She turns and lifts her face up to him.

The kiss is even better than she could have imagined. Brit loses herself in Jukka's arms and lets her body relax. He presses his lips against hers and begins to probe her mouth with his tongue. It's gentle at first, but then urgent, until they part, both panting.

'There's a great view from my bedroom too,' Jukka says hoarsely.

Brit cannot speak. Her desire has overtaken her body, rendering her unable to do anything but nod. Taking Jukka's proffered hand, she follows his tall shape into the bedroom beyond the darkened kitchen.

The bed is wide and covered in a fake fur throw. Jukka pushes Brit gently down into a sitting position and kneels in front of her for another kiss. Gently pushing her legs apart, he presses his body tight against hers. Brit touches his face, his hair, and neck, while Jukka places his hand on her breasts over the thin jumper. Again Brit cannot help but moan. Keeping his lips on hers, he quickly moves his hands to her back and finds the bra fastening. Swiftly, he unhooks the clasp, and leaning back slightly, pulls her jumper up and slowly, oh, so slowly, lowers each strap of her bra so that her upper body is naked. Jukka gazes at her erect nipples. 'You're beautiful,' he says, looking up at her eyes.

Brit is trembling. She wants Jukka to caress her so badly. Reaching out for his hand, she places it on her left breast and leans in for another kiss. Then, bringing Jukka with her, she gets up and begins to undo his jeans. He's already hard, and Brit wants to touch him.

Naked, they tumble onto the bed.

Afterward, when Brit is lying next to him on the bed, exhausted from their passion, he lifts himself up on his elbow and moves a strand of her hair behind her ear.

'I want to do this again?'

Brit smiles, 'What now?'

Jukka gazes down his naked body. He's certainly not ready yet, but Brit is so exciting, why not?

He says laughing, 'Not sure I can, but there's no harm in trying!'

Jukka bends down and begins to kiss her, but she stops him, 'I was joking!'

'You've got me going now,' he says and nods at the

area between his legs, where some movement is beginning to show.

They make love again, a little less hurried this time. Jukka has time to explore Brit's body more closely, which she seems to enjoy. He cannot remember when he's become so easily aroused by a woman. There is something strong, yet vulnerable about Brit. Her curvy body, firm breasts with their pink nipples, the partly shaved part between her legs, and her flat tummy and round buttocks would make any man go wild. But it's the way she occasionally takes charge during love-making, while moaning in his arms and waiting for him to act at other times, that raises his desire to an uncontrollable level. She's very good at giving him pleasure and her occasional whispers of 'Faster, faster,' reveal her enjoyment and spur him on.

After Jukka has taken Brit into his walk-in shower and gently soaped her whole body, they sit in front of the view again, with glasses of a rather good red wine. Jukka has given Brit the leather chair and pulled one of the seats that matches the gray settee in the lounge next to hers.

It makes Brit feel sad, but reassured, somehow, to see that there's just that one seat, with the matching small table made of light wood, facing the windows. All of Kerstin's snide remarks and hints about Jukka being a womanizer seem completely wrong.

Jukka gets up and walks the few steps into the kitchen, separated from the lounge by a half-wall. A narrow space, it's between Jukka's bedroom and the bathroom and sauna at the other end of the apartment. When Jukka took her into the shower, she had noticed that there was another bedroom facing the road. It had a neatly made up bed with a large, brown teddy bear sitting on it. She didn't want to ask, but she wondered if Jukka had children? Even though they had spent the early evening in bed, making love twice, it still seemed too personal a question. Or was it?

Brit glances toward Jukka, who is preparing spaghetti carbonara.

'My specialty,' he'd told her when he asked if she was hungry.

He's now standing at the stove, in bare feet, wearing a pair of jeans and a loose T-shirt over his wide shoulders. His hair is messy, which makes him look even more attractive.

I'm really falling for this guy.

Brit is starving, and the wine is making her even hungrier, so when Jukka returns with a large bowl of pasta and a fork, she thanks him and starts eating immediately. She tries to remain ladylike, but all the physical activity has given her a huge appetite.

FORTY

Patrick is wearing a white T-shirt with a pair of ripped blue jeans. His strong bare arms are still tanned from the summer, and covered in a thin layer of blond hair. He has his back to Alicia when she emerges from the elevator, which opens straight into his penthouse apartment. Alicia hasn't been inside his place since last August, when she was still reeling from their brief affair.

The apartment hasn't changed. There's still the incredible view across the sea from the open-plan living room, the same stylish pale gray sofas, the white kitchen and dining table at the back, and the vast seascape on the opposite wall, which almost matches the view from the windows. If the sea had been stormy rather than icy. Briefly, Alicia wonders how much the painting is worth, but puts aside such thoughts.

Patrick comes over and gives her an awkward one-armed hug, keeping his body inches away from her.

Alicia drinks in his scent, something expensive and

subtle. She has a sudden desire just to lean into his strong body and let go. Just stay there and forget about Frida, the baby, Dudnikov, Ebba, her mother and Uffe—and Liam. But she resists and pulls herself away.

He regards her briefly, but Alicia is trying to escape his scrutiny. She doesn't dare look at him and moves into the center of the room, where the two vast sofas face each other. She decides to sit down, then changes her mind and goes over to stand by the window.

Patrick goes back into the kitchen and returns with a wine glass.

'Red or white?'

'This isn't a social call,' Alicia says and places the glass on the smoked glass coffee table set on the white rug between the two sofas. She keeps her face straight.

Patrick sighs and sits down. She sees there's a glass of red wine on the table in front of him. She notices that his hair is wet. He looks as if he's just stepped out of the shower. He takes a sip of his drink and pulls the corners of his mouth into a smile. 'And here I was, hoping you'd decided to give the small island the heave ho and come with me to the big lights of Stockholm.'

'I need you to help with something, but if you won't …'

'Don't be like that. I'm impatient, that's all,' Patrick says and he comes to stand next to Alicia. He takes her hand and says, 'What's the problem?'

Alicia hesitates. She pulls her hand away from Patrick's. 'Perhaps I'll have that wine after all. I'm driving, so just the one glass. Red, please.'

'Coming up!'

While Patrick goes into the kitchen to fetch the bottle, Alicia sits down. She tries to decide how much she should tell him about Frida, the DNA test, Frida's mother, Sirpa Anttila's riches, and the Russian, Alexander Dudnikov. What does she really want him to do? Why is she really here?

She realizes that she wants to tell Patrick everything, and for him to help her make sense of it all. Should she tell him that Frida didn't have a baby with Stefan after all? A ping from her phone stops her train of thought. She reads the text displayed on the screen.

'*Where are you?*'

Alicia ignores her mother's message. She will have to deal with Hilda later. What will she say when she hears Anne Sofie is related to Dudnikov? And why is he still terrorizing them if he knows–which he must–that Frida's baby is his granddaughter? Alicia accepts the wine from Patrick, who sits next to her.

'So what's up?'

She looks him straight in the eyes. 'If I tell you something, you must promise not to use it to your own purposes.'

Patrick is quiet for a moment and then replies with a serious expression, 'Of course.'

'OK,' Alicia blows the air out of her lungs and says, 'I've just found out that Sirpa Anttila, Frida's mother, was wealthy.'

'Yeah I knew that.'

'What?'

'As did your lovely husband. I told him last summer when he came in asking whether Frida was after money.'

Before Alicia can take in what Patrick has just told her, her phone rings. She glances at it, expecting it to be Hilda. Alicia knows her mother was never going to let her messages go unanswered. But when she sees the name, Ebba, on her screen, she quickly presses the button to accept the call.

'Did you warn him off?'

Ebba sounds angry. Alicia can hear that she's somewhere windy, with loud engine noise in the background, and she immediately thinks, 'The airport'.

'Of course not!'

'Well, someone did.'

'What happened?' Alicia asks, adding quickly, 'I'm asking as a private person, not a journalist.'

Patrick's eyes shoot up when he hears Alicia's words.

'Hold on a moment,' Ebba says, and Alicia can hear the police chief talking to someone. She can't catch what they are saying.

'What's happening?' he mouths, but Alicia shakes her head and puts her hand up to silence him. She rises from the sofa and moves toward the vast windows, now overlooking a darkened sea. She can see lights, what she presumes is a vessel gliding slowly between sheets of ice in the shipping lane.

'Dudnikov boarded a private plane about an hour ago. According to air traffic control, the destination is Russia. St Petersburg to be more precise.'

Ebba pauses for a moment. 'So I ask you again, did you warn him off?'

'No,' Alicia replies. 'Why would I be sitting in your

office at the Police Headquarters telling you everything I knew if I didn't want him to be caught?'

There's a silence at the other end, and then in a tired voice, Ebba replies, 'Stranger things have happened. Anyway, I'm not able to do anything now. I'll pass all the information you supplied–such as it is, without accompanying evidence–to the Stockholm police. They can take it on from there. But you do know, don't you, that to get anyone extradited from Russia is a futile task?'

'Yes. I am aware. But how did you know where to find him?'

Ebba seems to hesitate for a moment, then says, 'I get the traffic movements to and from the islands in my routine reports each morning. A private plane traveling to Russia is always exceptional. I just put two and two together.' The police chief disconnects without saying another word and Alicia presses her forehead against the cool of the window pane. She hears Patrick moving behind her. Next, she feels his arms around her, and she hasn't got the strength to resist.

'Patrick,' she starts, but before she has time to utter the words, Patrick's mouth is on hers and she's again swept into his embrace, into the world that she thought she had left behind. His hands are on her hips and she can feel his hardness as he pulls her against him. Desire spreads through her body like wildfire, setting everything alight from between her legs to the tips of her fingers and toes.

FORTY-ONE

When, later that night, Brit is sitting in a taxi, on her way home, she checks her watch to see if it's too late to contact Alicia. She needs to tell someone about Jukka and the wonderful evening she's had with him.

'Guess where I've just been?'

When there's no reply, Brit hesitates for a moment, but decides to try phoning her friend. She feels like a teenager who's had sex for the first time and just has to confess—OK, brag!—about it. But after several rings, there's no reply. Instead she leaves a message on Alicia's answerphone.

'Ring me!'

It's not until the cab has pulled up outside her block of apartments that she gets a reply.

'Can't talk now, sorry.'

Brit is composing a reply while waiting for the elevator to her apartment, but when the doors open, she stops dead.

In the elevator, facing her stands Alicia. She looks just as surprised as Brit.

'I was just, what are you doing here?' Brit stammers.

Alicia is staring at her.

She looks guilty.

'Where have you been?'

Brit thinks back and realizes the panel had shown that the elevator was coming from the tenth floor, the penthouse apartment.

'Um, I was in the area and thought you might be at home. Your message sounded urgent.'

Brit harrumphs, raising a skeptical eyebrow and says, 'We both know that's not true.' She crosses her arms and when the elevator doors ping and begin to shut, she steps inside and presses the number of her own floor.

'Why don't you come in for a drink? It's nearly Christmas and I'm in love!'

Alicia sits at the kitchen table in Brit's apartment and holds her head in her hands. Brit, who was briefly annoyed when she stepped inside the lift, softened after Alicia told her about her eventful day. Besides, she's so happy herself that she's not capable of thinking badly of anyone.

'I've made such a mess of things!' Alicia lifts her head and Brit sees there are tears in her eyes.

'No you haven't. None of this is your fault,' Brit says and rubs her friends back. She's resting on her knees, next to her friend.

'I'll make you some coffee.'

'Thanks,' Alicia says and smiles sadly. 'Sleeping with Patrick is totally my fault. As was investigating the Russian. I should have just left it alone!'

'But the guy is a maniac. He tried to run your parents off the road and into the icy canal, remember? And you and me in Föglö. What was that but intimidation, pure and simple!'

'Yeah, I'm not sure if that was his way of introducing himself to his new family.'

Alicia lets out a short laugh and Brit, too, smiles at her words.

Brit puts a mug of hot, steaming coffee in front of Alicia, who takes a sip. 'I don't suppose you have anything stronger? It's been quite a day.'

'Now you're talking.'

While Brit goes to fetch a bottle of wine and glasses, Alicia glances at her phone. There are four more messages from her mother. She takes a deep breath and dials Hilda's number. She gets up and says to Brit, 'Just letting my mother know that I'm still alive.'

To say Hilda wasn't happy is an understatement. But Alicia reminds herself that she is a grown-up, a mother and a grandmother (or perhaps not?). But her mother was right about one thing. She needs to call Liam.

'Hi, I'm afraid I'm not going to make it back to Sjoland until much later,' Alicia says.

'I see,' Liam says. Alicia can hear anger in his voice. *He's got a nerve!*

'Well, I just thought I'd let you know.'

'Look, Alicia, I am going nuts in here. Your mother is fussing over me constantly, and there's no internet. I'm using 4G, which is so slow.'

'Look, you're grown-up. Call a cab and go into town, or go back to London. Frankly, I don't care what you do anymore.'

Alicia rings off. Hearing Liam whining about her mother has made her furious. Although thinking about it, she has completely abandoned him.

And he has betrayed me!

'Here's your wine,' Brit says, smiling. 'Everything alright at home?'

'Not really. But I don't care,' Alicia says and clinks glasses with her friend.

'I don't suppose you could let me stay tonight?'

The two friends drink wine and talk into the night. Brit tells Alicia about Jukka, his incredible apartment, and their love-making.

'It was just amazing.'

Alicia takes her friend's hand and says, 'I'm so glad for you. You deserve a good man after, you-know-who.'

'Don't say his name! I don't want to think about him,' Brit interrupts her.

Alicia tells Brit everything. She recounts how Liam had stolen a piece of hair from little Anne Sofie, as well as from the envelope where Alicia had saved her son's locks. And how he thought that the DNA test result would be a relief to her.

'He actually thinks that I don't want to be Anne Sofie's grandmother!'

'So that's why you slept with Patrick tonight?' Brit asks.

Her friend's question takes Alicia by surprise. Is that what she was doing?

'No!' she says, but she isn't sure if her friend hasn't just put her finger on it. Is she using Patrick?

Again?

When he'd asked her whether she had thought about Stockholm, she'd been evasive. Truthfully, she replied that she hadn't had time, but she knew, really, that she hadn't considered the move as a serious proposal. Why? Because she is fairly certain she wants to stay on the islands.

Brit puts her hands up. 'You are a free woman. Believe me, men don't mind why you have sex with them. As long as you do.'

They both laugh, but afterward both sink into their own thoughts, looking out of the windows at the empty blackness. The two friends are sitting on a plush sofa. Brit's apartment is the same layout as Patrick's upstairs, with the same views.

Alicia isn't sure whether what Brit just said applies to Patrick. Or Liam, for that matter.

FORTY-TWO

Driving home in the dim light of the morning, Alicia feels terrible. The landscape around her is stunning, with snow banks on either side of the road and hanging heavy on the pine trees. There are no vehicles on the road; it's not even seven o'clock on Christmas Eve. The shops in the center of town will open for just a couple of hours this morning and the offices have already shut their doors for the holidays.

When she comes to the road running along East Harbor, she thinks how dramatically different it looks with snow and the frozen water. The East Harbor doesn't lead straight to the open waters, but is protected by a piece of land jutting out—Sjoland. Smaller vessels from mainland Finland enter from this side of the islands, but they must first cross the Sjoland Canal, which shuts during icy winters.

As Alicia nears the swing bridge, she finds herself hoping Uffe has cleared the fresh snow from the drive down to her sauna cottage. She wants to creep in unnoticed. She needs a large cup of coffee and some time to think.

What am I going to do?

She's had a number of messages from Patrick, asking for her to call him. But she can't. She feels she's betrayed both Liam and Patrick with her actions last night. But she struggles to ignore the warm feeling she has inside. Patrick's touch, his body, the way she melted into his arms, made her the happiest she's been since the previous summer, at the beginning of their affair. Then, Patrick ignited something inside Alicia, something that she cannot ignore. But is that just carnal passion? Just sex, not love? Is this what Liam felt for the Polish nurse? A relationship he ended and now says he can forget?

Whatever Brit says about men, she has the feeling that Patrick isn't like that. Perhaps he was once, but not anymore. Besides, she wouldn't want to be with a man who doesn't think going to bed with a woman means anything more but just the act. Or does she?

Alicia slept badly at Brit's place. She dreamed about Anne Sofie being taken by a faceless man. Frida had been there but she'd just smiled at Alicia and said, 'It's for the best, you know it is.'

During the night she decided she would never tell Frida that she was aware of Dudnikov's disappearance. Or that she knew him. She knows it wasn't her fault that Dudnikov left the islands. The permissions for the private plane to fly from Mariehamn to St Petersburg had been sought well before Alicia went to see Ebba. The police's sudden dash after Dudnikov hadn't make him flee the islands. That proves it had nothing to do with Alicia. Still, her aim was to get the Russian behind bars. Thinking about everything she has done and been through during the last few days makes her mouth go dry. And there's a headache building between her eyes.

She's relieved to see the road down to the cottage has been cleared and the lights in the house are off, apart from Hilda's Christmas star lanterns, which shine brightly out of the dark panes of the downstairs windows and reflect on the snow outside.

When Alicia unlocks the door to the cottage, she can see there's a shape in her bed. Liam's feet are peeking out of the duvet. His legs are too long for the small sofa bed in the cottage. His dark hair is in stark contrast to the white of the sheets, but Alicia can't see his face because he's got his back toward her.

She closes the door behind her silently, and tiptoes around the lightless room. She doesn't want a confrontation with Liam until she's had time to think, and calm down, but she has nowhere else to go. Being challenged by Hilda would be worse, so going up to the main house isn't an option. Besides, if Hilda is awake, she'll have seen Alicia's car drive down to the cottage and will be in touch immediately.

Alicia seats herself in one of the chairs facing the small window. It's still dark, the sun isn't going to come up for another two hours, but there's a faintest of lights on the horizon behind the pine trees, which are heavy with snow. It's from one of the small islands opposite. It amazes Alicia what a difference the snowfall has made to the light even at night. She's forgotten how it illuminates the landscape. It's as if the sun plants lightbulbs in the snow during the day only to be switched on as twilight settles over the country. 'Solar powered snow,' Alicia thinks to herself and lets out a small chuckle. It's chilly in the room, and Alicia thinks she needs to relight the fire in the wood burner in the corner of the room.

Over in the bed, Liam stirs, and immediately Alicia regrets making a sound. She gazes over Liam's tall shape underneath the covers, and as her eyes wander toward his head, she sees he's awake and watching her. For a moment both stare at each other. Liam's eyes are sleepy, and his hair is ruffled. Self-consciously, he runs his hand through it.

'Good morning,' he says and his voice sounds hoarse.

'Hi,' Alicia replies.

Neither move for what seems like a very long time to Alicia.

Finally, she decides to break the silence and asks, 'Coffee?'

Liam is regretting his stupid decision to go to bed naked. He was drunk last night and planned on seducing Alicia as soon as she came home. But then he fell asleep and now, on waking, he sees from the large clock fixed to the little kitchenette in the corner of the room that it's already nearly eight in the morning. Although it's still dark outside. Why do people want to live in this harsh climate? Or more particularly, why does Alicia want to live here? Surely the knowledge that she's not Anne Sofie's grandmother after all, and the experience of her first cold, dark winter on these godforsaken islands in nearly twenty years, is enough to make her realize that her home is in London?

Liam is dying for a pee, but in order to reach the loo, he has to walk across the room, right past Alicia, who's measuring coffee into a percolator. And all his clothes are in a pile on one of the chairs at the end of the bed. Too far to walk without Alicia seeing the state of him.

The sight of Alicia, who's standing in her tight jeans with her back to him, with her round buttocks at eye level, doesn't do anything to reduce his morning glory.

'I thought you might sleep in the main house?' Alicia says, not turning toward him. Is there an accusation in the remark, or is she making general conversation? Liam can't tell, but fears it's the former. She's now bending down in front of the log burner, crunching newspaper into balls and laying logs on top of them. She lights the fire with matches and stands up, gazing at him.

She doesn't want me here.

'Look, Alicia. Can we talk?' he says.

Alicia sighs. She's standing in front of the now blazing fire. She looks tired and somehow disheveled and suddenly Liam knows where she's spent the night. No, surely she wouldn't? Not when her husband is actually here, on the islands? When in London, rattling around the large house in Crouch End on his own, his jealousy sometimes takes such a firm hold in the night that he has to fight the urge to phone Alicia, just to check she's not in bed with him, that self-satisfied Swede. Liam thinks he would be able to tell just from hearing her voice, without having to lose his dignity and actually ask her.

'Sure,' she says wearily.

Liam's fury is mounting, but he tries to calm himself. It may not be what he thinks. He has been wrong before. Plus he is hungover, so his mental faculties aren't in peak condition. At least the thought of Alicia in bed with Patrick enables him to get out of bed without embarrassment.

Alicia gasps, surprised by his naked body, but now Liam doesn't care. He's her husband after all! And he's perfectly flaccid, and it's not as if she's never seen him naked before. Although it's several years since they shared a bedroom. Even last year when they slept in the attic room in Hilda's house, he remembers how they both undressed in the bathroom.

What is he playing at, Alicia wonders. She gets that he didn't want to arouse Hilda's suspicions by asking to stay in the main house, although that's what she had hoped for, but his nakedness speaks another truth.

Alicia remembers when their sex life was still normal, one of the ways they would indicate that they wanted to make love was to go to bed naked. If she did this and Liam was working late, which he often was, he would wake her up, if she'd fallen asleep, by kissing her neck. Liam would do the same, if on a rare occasion a news story took Alicia out in the evening and he was in bed before her.

While she's watching Liam pull his boxer shorts and jeans on, she realizes that when she was swamped by work, he wanted to make love to her all the time. Her independence and passion for journalism turned him on.

But she wasn't happiest then. Yes, she liked working for a large busy newspaper, but she also found it immensely stressful. She hated being away from Stefan and not being there when he came home from school. Motherhood to her was the best job in the world. It wasn't what the modern woman was supposed to want, but it was what she adored.

Liam turns around. He's found an old T-shirt to wear, and his hands are on his hips. His expression is fierce, something Alicia hasn't seen before.

'Did you sleep with him last night?'

Liam's question feels like a slap across her face.

'That's none of your business,' she says.

Liam is staring at her. He's still standing across the room from her, framed by the dimmed window behind him. His eyes are black, like the sky outside. Suddenly Alicia feels an anger emanating from him that makes her want to flee the cottage.

'In other words, you did. How could you? When I'm actually here!' Liam has raised his voice. He takes a step toward Alicia, who wraps her arms around her body. The gesture makes Liam stop and he sits down in the chair where moments ago his clothes were in a messy heap. He puts his head in his hands.

Alicia doesn't know what to do. She turns back to the log burner. The fire is steady, so she closes the doors and briefly warms her hands against the stove. The coffee percolator makes its final gurgling sounds and stops. With shaking hands, Alicia takes two mugs from the hooks Uffe has fixed onto the wall above the little sink and pours coffee for both of them.

She goes over to where Liam is sitting and places the cups on a table between the two comfy chairs and then lowers herself into one of them. The armrests are worn. All the furniture in the cottage is from the seventies. The chairs are angular and the table has legs that inconveniently jut out beyond the wooden top. It's a style that is coming back into fashion, but Alicia has always loved it. It reminds her of her childhood. The cottage has been the same ever since she can remember and she wouldn't change it for anything. It's a wonder Hilda has let it be, Alicia thinks, and a smile forms on her lips.

'Funny, is it?' Liam says.

He picks up his mug of coffee and takes a swig. Almost immediately he splutters, 'Shit!'

'It's hot,' Alicia says.

Liam gives her a murderous look.

'For your information I was thinking how this cottage hasn't changed in forty years, and how strange that is, given my mother's love of renewing and remodeling everything.'

Now Liam is staring at her.

'You're unbelievable.'

'Sorry, I'm really tired. And so much has happened I can't quite keep my head straight.'

'You think?' Liam says in his most sarcastic tone.

Alicia sighs again and gets up, holding onto her coffee.

'If you are interested in what is happening in my life, rather than just worried about your male pride, we can have a conversation. You and I haven't been married—in its true sense—for years now, have we?'

Liam is looking down at the floor, but then lifts his head. 'OK. I agree, but I love you, Alicia. Isn't that clear? I'm here, aren't I?'

Alicia walks back to the chair and sits down. It's true, Liam is here, he is making an effort. But what for? To get her back to London at all costs?

She places a hand over Liam's. His long fingers with the neat, manicured fingernails and the dark hairs growing between the knuckles are so familiar, yet touching him now seems weird, different somehow. She looks at his face, the contours of which she knows intimately. Perhaps there are a few more wrinkles around his eyes and mouth, but his face and dark eyes with the long lashes are so familiar that she wonders how it can be that she finds him so distant now.

'Yes, you are here now. But you are not taking into consideration what I want. Just what *you* want from me,' Alicia says softly.

She's keeping her eyes on Liam's eyes and continues, 'If you are willing to listen, I can tell you what that is.'

FORTY-THREE

Brit is frustrated. All the previous evening, Alicia talked about her life, which Brit has to agree, is more than complicated at the moment, but her preoccupation meant that she didn't have a chance to tell her much about Jukka. And this morning, her friend dashed off before waking her, only leaving a note to say she needed to get back to Sjoland. Brit wanted so desperately to tell someone how incredibly, deliriously happy Jukka is making her.

Brit is now enjoying a leisurely breakfast, while wondering what Jukka is doing. Buying last-minute Christmas presents, no doubt. Brit is all ready, she just needs to do a bit of wrapping, take a cab into town to collect her car, and drive to Föglö to fetch her father. They are due at the Ulssons' house at 5pm, so she has plenty of time.

During a brief moment when she and Alicia were not discussing Alicia's life last night, Brit said that she feared

Jukka was going to be alone for the holidays. Alicia had immediately said he was welcome at Hilda and Uffe's.

'It's a bit early for spending Christmas together,' Brit had replied, but now she thinks it might be a brilliant idea. She knows Jukka is on call with Marie Line, but he can always drive to Sjoland and then take a cab home if need be.

Although their relationship is very new, she already knows how she feels about him. She's more serious about him than she expected. Even when he was driving her to his home yesterday—and she knew what was to happen when they arrived in Solbacken—she'd considered it to be casual. But, unlike the other brief affairs she's had, the love-making with Jukka had been real somehow, better. Their bodies were in perfect sync, and the way he acted afterward, all gentle and considerate, cooking her a meal and making sure she was safe in the cab afterward, spoke to her more than words. He's also smitten with her, she's fairly sure of it.

Brit lifts her arms above her head and stretches.

How wonderful it is to be in love again.

Brit's happy thoughts are interrupted by a buzzing sound. Her telephone next to the coffee cup lights up with an incoming call. The display shows, 'Unknown number,' but Brit picks up anyway. It may be Jukka's home phone. Perhaps they are so in tune already, she muses, that when she thinks about him, he also has her in his mind.

'Hi Brit, this is Kerstin Eklund,' the voice at the other end says.

For a moment Brit has to think who on earth it is, but then she realizes.

'Hi, what can I do for you?' Brit asks, trying to sound professional and not showing her annoyance. Doesn't the woman know it's not the done thing to telephone a member of the crew when they are not on duty? On Christmas Eve? Brit isn't even on call like Jukka.

There is a brief silence at the other end and Brit thinks they've lost the connection.

'Hello?' she says and hears the woman clear her throat.

'You need to know something.'

Brit listens for more, but when the woman is quiet, she replies, 'Yes,' again, trying not to show her irritation.

'Our Captain Jukka Markusson has a murky past. Before you two get all loved up, I think it's only fair someone should warn you.'

Brit has stopped breathing. What is this woman talking about?

'Hello, are you there?' she hears Kerstin say.

'Yes,' Brit manages to reply.

'Look him up on the internet. Especially stories from two years back.'

The line goes dead.

Brit paces up and down her apartment. She knows Kerstin doesn't like Jukka, or her for that matter. It was perfectly clear from day one when she stepped onboard the ship and was shown around by the older woman. But surely she can't be jealous? Kerstin is nearly at retirement age, past sixty, some twenty years older than Jukka. No, the animosity must stem from something else. Perhaps she's just one of those bitter women who blame what they lack in life on others? But if there is nothing to worry about, Brit will find nothing bad about Jukka on the web, surely?

She opens her laptop and puts Jukka's name in the search box. Why she hasn't done this before, is beyond her. Surely she should have searched the web well before now. Her heart is pounding when she sees the first page on the listing, which is the Marie Line's official website. An image of him wearing freshly pressed uniform and cap fills the screen when she taps on the link. There is nothing there, just an article from a five-year-old annual statement regarding career progression.

Brit goes back to the page listing all the sites containing Jukka's name and finds an article from two years ago that has the caption, 'Captain investigated for sexual harassment onboard a Marie Line ferry.'

Brit scans the article from *Ålandsbladet* quickly.

There is an internal investigation taking place inside one of the island's premier ferry operators, Marie Line, against Captain Jukka Markusson, who has been accused of sexual harassment by an employee, Ms Sia Eklund. Ms Eklund claims that Captain Markusson touched her inappropriately on several occasions and made sexual advances while she worked as a cabin attendant onboard MS Viking. No criminal charges have been brought against Markusson, but Ms Eklund tells Ålandsbladet, *'If nothing comes out of this investigation, I will take the matter up with the police.'*

.   .   .

Brit starts to look frantically for any further reports, but finds only one small item, in the same paper:

The Marie Line investigation on sexual harassment charges brought by Ms Eklund have been completed.

There is no mention of Jukka, nor what the outcome was. Then it hits her. Ms Eklund. Is that Kerstin's daughter? Brit tries to wrack her brain. Did the older woman mention having a daughter?

Brit finds herself shaking.

FORTY-FOUR

Patrick is restless. He's sent two messages to Alicia but she hasn't replied to either of them. She fled in such a hurry last night that Patrick doesn't know what she is thinking. And he knows that her husband is in Sjoland, waiting to pounce on her with his news about Frida's baby and his conviction that she should go back to London with him. He cannot let that happen. He's already been in limbo with Alicia for six months now and he cannot take anymore.

At first, he thought he could manage to be just friends with her; he could wait. But over the months, weeks and days they shared the same office, her close presence became more and more torturous to him. He kept dreaming about having her in his arms, about their love-making, which was always so thrilling, so all-consuming. When she asked him to go and clear the snow from Hilda and Uffe's house, he thought that was some kind of change in their relationship. That she wanted to see him out of the office, as much as he longed to be with her.

And then last night—surely what happened changes everything?

With Mia and the girls away for Christmas, Patrick was planning to spend the holidays in front of the telly, eating the lobster he'd bought at the fish market yesterday morning. He has a magnum bottle of vintage champagne, and planned to get himself anesthetized until the festivities were over.

But now, he can't bring himself to even open the bottle, nor can he concentrate on anything, not even the new PlayStation games he got for the two days he would be spending on his own. (He had used the excuse that the girls would love to play with him on their return from their skiing holiday to Sweden.)

Patrick makes a decision. He glances at his watch. He has a couple of hours before the shops close. He puts on his jacket and rushes out of the door.

FORTY-FIVE

'So what is it you want?' Liam says and runs his palm across his face. His eyes are full of sleep and Alicia thinks he looks at least as weary as she feels, if not more.

'First, can I tell you what's been going on?'

Liam nods and Alicia tells him about Dudnikov, how he's been terrorizing Hilda, and how he nearly ran her parents and her off the road.

Liam leans over the small table. He puts a hand on Alicia's thigh.

'Why didn't you tell me any of this? You must have been frightened.'

Suddenly Alicia feels tearful. How easy it would be to let Liam comfort her. Let him take charge of everything again just as he did after they lost Stefan, and almost from the start, when they met in Uppsala all those years ago.

But then she remembers how he, stubbornly, has been driving his own agenda. How he betrayed her for months with that nurse, leaving her alone in their bed at night while he slept in the spare bedroom. She knows she was to blame too, a little at least. She's surprised to find that she no longer feels anger toward Liam. Just sadness that it's now all over.

'It's OK,' she says. And looking at Liam's concerned face. 'The complication in all this is that I also found out yesterday that Dudnikov is Frida's father.'

Liam leans back in his chair, removing his hand and blowing air out of his mouth.

There's an emptiness where his touch was, but the sensation comes almost as a relief to Alicia.

'Right,' Liam says and glances at her.

She knows exactly what he's thinking.

'He's also been supporting Frida's mother, Sirpa, all these years and there's a bit of a nest egg left over for Frida and Anne Sofie.'

Liam nods, still keeping his eyes on Alicia. She remembers that Patrick told her Liam knew Frida's mother was wealthy.

'But then you knew that, didn't you?'

Liam's eyes widen.

'All I knew was that Frida wasn't poor, your know-it-all Swedish boyfriend told me that,' he says.

Alicia ignores Liam's jibe. Instead, she explains how she felt she needed to tell the police chief about Dudnikov, to protect Hilda and Uffe, but that she doesn't want Frida to know.

'Or anyone else, for that matter.'

'Sure, I can see that,' Liam says.

They agree that they will not mention any of this over Christmas.

'How does Patrick fit into all of this?' Liam spits out his name although he speaks quietly, calm now.

'He doesn't,' Alicia says. 'And I don't know what to think about him—or me,' she adds, looking down at her hands.

While they have been sitting in the sauna cottage talking, the light has changed in the room. Suddenly a ray of sunshine penetrates through the small panes of glass, and Alicia peers out, almost blinded by the sight.

'Look at that!'

Liam turns his head toward the window behind him.

'What about Anne Sofie?' he asks softly, not looking at Alicia.

'I haven't told Frida about your little test, if that's what you mean,' Alicia says, trying to keep her anger at bay. She still cannot understand how Liam thought it would help her to know that the baby isn't Stefan's. But it doesn't matter now.

'But both Frida and the baby are OK? Financially speaking, I mean?' Liam asks.

'It's not all about money,' Alicia says drily.

'Of course not, but having it helps,' Liam replies quickly.

Alicia nods. She gets up and, looking toward the bed, says, 'Perhaps it would be better if you sleep in the main house tonight.'

Liam widens his eyes, 'Alone, you mean?'

Alicia sits down on top of the rumbled bedsheets. 'Liam, I'm sorry, but I think we've come to the end of the road. Don't you?'

'Is this because of the DNA test?' Liam asks. He's

trying to keep himself calm, even though he can feel his pulse is sky high. Just as well he has low cholesterol levels and a good, strong heart.

Clinically speaking, that is.

He's still wearing yesterday's underwear, jeans, and the old T-shirt he usually sleeps in. He longs for a shower, a good breakfast (what he would give for a full English, bacon and eggs and all the works, at this moment). But more than that, what he really wants to do is take Alicia into his arms and make love to her. Unwittingly, he glances at the bed, unmade and messy, in front of him. He sees from the corner of his eye that Alicia has seen where his gaze has landed.

She sighs and says, in that new, cold voice that he has come to know well over the past six months, 'Liam, you know we haven't been a proper couple for years.'

And there it is.

His own mistake is what has got him here.

'You know I've forgiven you for what happened last summer.' Liam stops when he hears the pathetic pleading in his voice. He feels like a dying man who's trying to get a last-minute reprieve. But before Alicia has time to interrupt, he carries on, trying to make his voice sound stronger and more confident. 'I know I am the one who made the biggest mistake. And I am truly sorry. I don't know why I did it. It was stupid and unforgivable. But to throw away eighteen years of marriage, isn't there something out of those wonderful times together that we can salvage?'

Alicia is gazing at him and he can see that she has tears in her eyes.

Liam stands and goes to kneel before her. Taking her hands into his, he says, 'Please, Alicia, don't give up on us yet.'

'I want a divorce.'

Liam is staring at Alicia, but his face looks resigned.

'I see,' he says quietly and looks away from Alicia. He fidgets with his empty coffee mug, but says nothing more.

There is a long silence, which Alicia is tempted to break on several occasions. She looks at his familiar shape, his chin where a stubble is growing. His long, bare feet and his strong arms and legs.

On one level she still loves Liam more than she can let him know now, but the love is more like that for a brother, perhaps. Having never had siblings, she doesn't know how that feels but she imagines this is what it's like. He can be infuriating, and she is still angry with him over the baby's DNA test, but she finds now that she has forgiven him.

Seeing his empty coffee cup, she wants to ask him if he'd like more, but she stays quiet. She knows she has to let Liam take in her statement in his own time and on his own terms.

Finally, Liam lifts his face up and asks, 'Do you want me to leave today?'

'No, goodness, no!' Alicia says, almost too emphatically. 'Besides, there are no flights or ferries to the mainland today, I'm fairly sure of it.'

'OK,' Liam says simply.

Relieved that he's taken the news so calmly, Alicia adds, 'Do you want some more coffee?'

. . .

Alicia picks up some clothes from a rail she's put up in one corner of the cottage and gets changed in the shower room. She can hear Liam taking up the sofa-bed and moving furniture. She wants to go and hug him, but she doesn't want to send the wrong signals. She's surprised how calm Liam was when she told him she didn't want to be married to him anymore. There was none of the drama from last year, when he'd turned up unannounced and caught Patrick and Alicia in bed in this very same cottage—one of the reasons she'd been so surprised to find him sleeping there naked this morning.

He must have been quite drunk.

But that's all over now. She has finally made the decision that she should have made months ago, perhaps even years ago. The relief she feels is such that she actually finds herself smiling. She pulls out her phone and sees Patrick's messages. She types a reply, and begins to think about Christmas dinner. Hilda must be going frantic with all the last-minute preparations without her. Alicia rushes out of the bathroom, but finds the sauna cottage empty. From a small side window, she sees her soon to be ex-husband walking toward the main house, taking long strides across the snow.

FORTY-SIX

When she walks up to the main house, the view could be from a Hans Andersen fairy tale. The sun is low on the horizon, behind a layer of clouds, giving the landscape a yellow hue. The strange light makes Hilda's minimal decorations of the house, with the star lanterns in the windows and the pine tree strung with fairy lights in the yard, look wonderful. Alicia begins to get the Christmas feeling she thought she would never again experience after Stefan. How he would have loved this family celebration!

As soon as Alicia steps into the main house, she hugs her mother and wishes her *God Jul.*

'Happy Christmas to you too!' Hilda is smiling but Alicia can hear that that her voice is strained. She's stressed over the day.

'What can I do?' Alicia says and the two women begin to go over Hilda's lists, with the day's meals and activities, including when to light the real candles on the indoor tree. Alicia looks over to the lounge, where an enormous spruce is standing, its tip almost touching the ceiling.

'Will you decorate it later?' Hilda asks before they begin going through Hilda's Christmas agenda.

'Of course. It's all going to be wonderful,' Alicia says and she squeezes her mother's hand. 'You've done so much already!'

Hilda beams. After the two women have decided what still needs to be done and by whom, Alicia's mother glances over at Liam, who's sitting in the lounge, his eyes fixed on the screen of his reading device.

'Everything OK?' she asks Alicia in a low voice. Her eyes are full of concern and Alicia wonders how much she knows, or has guessed, about her and Liam's relationship.

'Don't worry, all is well,' Alicia says.

'In that case, I think it's time for a drink!'

Sitting around the kitchen table, beautifully dressed with a red linen cloth and four Advent candles in a holder decorated with reindeer moss and red berries, Hilda, Uffe, Liam and Alicia eat rice pudding, the traditional Christmas Eve lunch. Hilda cuts up some ham and they discuss whether it's too salty, or perhaps not salty enough? It's what happens every year. Uffe offers Liam a beer, but he refuses.

Alicia smiles at him and says, 'Peaked a bit too early, did you?'

Liam gives a short laugh, and nods to Uffe. 'I think I will have one after all.'

Uffe gets his meaning without Alicia having to translate the English, and opens a bottle for him.

In the middle of the meal, Alicia gets a call from Brit.

'Can I pop over on my way to get my dad from Föglö? I need to talk to you about something urgently.'

'Come to the sauna cottage, we can talk better there,' Alicia says.

Hilda gives Alicia a look, and Alicia mouths, 'Brit,' to her.

Half an hour later Brit gets out of her car and waves to Alicia, who opens the door. She's in her padded coat and snow boots, but she still manages to look glamorous. How does she do it, Alicia wonders. Brit has bright red lipstick, which matches the bobble on her woolly hat, as well as her nails. Her face is made up, although in an understated way, apart from her lips.

'You look nice,' Alicia says and hugs her friend. 'And thank you for last night, I don't know what I would have done without you!'

Brit extracts herself from Alicia's arms and waves her manicured hand, 'My pleasure. It's so nice to have you living so close. Now we can have these girly nights in!'

Alicia smiles and asks, 'Coffee?'

'Please! It's started snowing again. When will it ever stop?'

'Don't knock it, it's wonderful to have a white Christmas.'

Brit nods and sits down on the sofa.

'Listen, I've seen something awful about Jukka online.'

Alicia examines the articles Brit shows her on her mobile phone. 'That's what, two years ago?'

'Yes, but look what he's been accused of? And then there's nothing to say what happened. Did he do it, or what? I don't know what to think. I've been going crazy at home. At first I thought I'd phone him, but then I didn't know what to say. How am I going to tell him that the woman, Kerstin, shopped him to me? How would I know about it otherwise? And they work together. I don't want him to think that I've been stalking him online! But I think the woman who was accusing him may have been her daughter.' Brit's eyes are wide and she is speaking so quickly that Alicia has to concentrate hard to understand her.

'Slow down, who told you about this?'

Finally, Alicia gets all the facts straight. She fetches her laptop and checks *Ålandsbladet's* archives, but finds nothing more than what Brit already saw online.

'I think you need to talk to him,' Alicia says.

'That's what I think too, but I don't want to do it over the phone. And now it's Christmas Eve and I'm late picking Dad up already.' Brit glances at Alicia and adds, 'Plus I don't trust myself with men anymore. What if he swears there was nothing to it, and I believe him. And then the next thing that happens is that he turns into—or turns out to be—a total rat?'

Alicia doesn't know what to say. She wants to tell Brit that, with only two serious relationships in her life, she's hardly one to give advice on how to tell if a lover is truthful or not.

But Brit doesn't seem to want her to respond. Instead

she says, 'I wondered,' here she hesitates for a moment, bites her lower lip, and then continues, 'Jukka is on call this Christmas, but because none of the ferries start operating until the 26th, he's basically off for the whole holiday. He's on his own in Solbacken, so I wondered if your mother and Uffe might be able to invite him over tonight after all?'

Alicia is again speechless. She knows her mother would certainly not mind having another guest. Her motto for any celebration is, 'The more the merrier.' And there's so much food, they could feed the five thousand. Adding a sea captain to the guest lists would certainly please Hilda.

When she doesn't reply, Brit goes on, 'The thing is, you and your mother, who I know is an excellent judge of character, could check him out and tell me what you think!' Brit is smiling now, 'Please, will you have him?'

Alicia returns her friend's smile. 'I'm sure it'll be fine. He might have to get a cab home, though. We're running out of rooms!'

Brit flings her arms around Alicia and thanks her so many times that Alicia has to tell her to stop. She waves Brit goodbye from the side window, and shaking her head, checks on the fire in the cottage, and follows her out, shutting the door behind her. She can't wait to tell Hilda the good news.

FORTY-SEVEN

'Markusson,' Uffe says rubbing his chin. 'That name rings a bell.'

Hilda and Alicia are standing in the kitchen, waiting. Uffe knows everybody on the islands, something her mother and Alicia often laugh about. When he doesn't say anything else, and picks up a paper, Alicia assumes Jukka's family isn't known to him after all.

'Anyway, he's welcome! The more the merrier and he can talk to Liam in English and keep him company.'

Hearing his name being mentioned, Liam looks up from his iPad.

He's got no problems getting on the internet today.

'We've got yet another guest for supper tonight, and Hilda thinks he'll be good company for you,' Alicia translates for Liam.

He nods and goes back to his iPad.

Alicia smiles at her mother, who is always worrying about Liam. She puts her arm around Hilda and says,

'That's true, but you mustn't worry about him. He'll be fine.'

Hilda's eyes meet hers, 'Well, he's still a guest in this house.'

Alicia checks if Liam has heard her, or understood the Swedish, which she knows he hasn't. Sometimes, however, he has a sixth sense about what's being said. But Liam has his head bent over the device. Suddenly, Uffe's voice booms over the house.

'I've got it!' her stepfather says, putting one finger up in the air. 'Ville Markusson was a nasty piece of work. A sailor and a drunk. He was never at home, but when he deigned to see his family, he knocked his wife about something awful. She was a Finn. Pirkko, I think she was called. Everybody, including old Pirkko, were pretty relieved when he kicked the bucket somewhere abroad. But the old girl died soon after, probably tired of life, leaving young Jukka alone. I think he's a sea captain now?'

'That's a terrible story,' Hilda exclaims. 'Not something we want to talk about on Christmas Eve!'

Now Liam is looking at the three of them. He's worked out that they're talking about something serious. Alicia puts her hand up to Liam and moves closer to Uffe, who's sitting at the opposite end of the room from Liam, in one of the many armchairs in the large lounge.

'Are you sure it's the same family?' she asks Uffe, who's gone back to his paper.

He lowers his reading glasses and looks over them. 'Yes, I'm fairly sure. If the boy is a sea captain?'

'He is. On Marie Line.'

'That's the right family then.'

'How do you know them?' Alicia asks.

Uffe folds his paper and balances it on one of his knees. He takes off his glasses and regards Alicia, as if to consider whether he should tell her the story. Alicia waits.

Uffe sighs.

'Well, I knew Ville at school. He was a little bully then. A year or two younger than me, but still, he tried to land one on me. I gave him what for and he didn't bother me after that. But I believe he beat up the pupils in the classes below him. Often in trouble with the teachers. A naughty boy who grew into a nasty man.'

'Stop talking about such unpleasant matters.' Hilda comes over to where Alicia is standing. She's wearing her red and white Christmas apron with rows of snowflakes and reindeer interspersed with hearts. Brandishing a wooden mixing spoon, she adds, 'He's welcome here to celebrate with us. I've got plenty of food. But mind, don't be talking about his family when he's here. We don't want to embarrass the poor boy.' Hilda points the spoon at Uffe, who harrumphs, opens the paper, and pulls it up to cover his face.

Alicia wonders how domestic violence can be more 'embarrassing' than tragic.

'Surely you mean, you don't want to upset him?' she cannot help commenting on her mother's words.

'Yes, yes, whatever.' Hilda waves her hand at Alicia.

'Now, we'd better get on if we are to have anything ready by 5pm for all this crowd to eat!'

'Wait,' Alicia says. She follows Hilda into the kitchen, and in a low voice says, 'I wanted to tell you that Dudnikov won't be bothering you two anymore.'

'What do you mean?' Hilda says, so loudly that Alicia is afraid Uffe will hear. She hasn't spoken directly with Uffe about the Russians and she doesn't want to start now. The less she knows about what has been going on between her stepfather and Dudnikov, the better. She doesn't want to have to lie to Ebba, who might wish to investigate the Russian's activities on the islands further. She hopes that the police chief doesn't know that her parents, or at least her mother, was a victim of that man. It would just complicate everything.

'Shh,' Alicia says, putting her finger to her lips. She points with the head to the lounge, where the two men are reading.

'Aah,' Hilda says and leans toward Alicia.

'He fled the islands in a private plane to St Petersburg yesterday. That was one of the reasons why I was so busy.'

Hilda's eyes widen, 'Good riddance!' she says, again raising her voice. 'You're not writing about him, are you,' Hilda says more quietly now.

Alicia shakes her head. She looks into the lounge through the little serving hatch Hilda installed when she remodeled the house, but both men remain engrossed in their reading, so she continues, 'No, of course not. I don't want anything more to do with him.'

Hilda has tears in her eyes and puts her arms around Alicia.

'You're a good girl,' she says.

FORTY-EIGHT

Jukka arrives carrying a massive bouquet of flowers. They are bright red roses.

'Where did you get all of these?' Hilda exclaims, clearly delighted with the gift.

Jukka gives a short laugh. He glances at Brit, who is standing in the hall behind Hilda. Brit has left her father with Uffe. The two know each other from years back, but don't move in the same circles anymore. They have a lot to catch up on.

'I think I emptied out the City Blommor on Torggatan.'

'I should think so,' Hilda says, her head half-buried behind the greenery. 'Lilly would have made sure she didn't have any stock remaining over the two-day holiday, so you were lucky.'

'Hello,' Jukka says and moves closer to Brit for an embrace. But before his mouth touches Brit's lips, she shifts her head sideways, so that his kiss lands on her cheek. She didn't plan to do it, but suddenly, she couldn't face such intimacy with him.

Before she'd left Alicia in Sjoland to make her way to the Föglö ferry, she messaged Jukka to ask if he'd like to join the Ulsson family for Christmas Eve. He took a long time to reply, but when she was disembarking in Föglö, her phone showed an incoming call from him.

Brit did feel bad about lying to him, pretending that her only motive was that she didn't want him to be alone in his apartment, however wonderful the view was. The result justifies the means, she thought. And then, to her huge surprise, he agreed.

Now she feels like she's hatched some kind of trap for him. When the three women saw his car pull up the drive, Hilda said, conspiratorially, 'Alicia, you stay here, and Brit and I will go and meet him in the hall.' She undid her red apron and fluffed up her hair. 'I'll just nip into the bathroom to check my makeup.'

'Your mother's not going to overdo it, is she?' Brit whispered to Alicia when Hilda was out of earshot.

'I'm sure she'll be cool,' Alicia said, though she didn't look at all certain.

'Come and meet the others,' Brit now says and takes Jukka's hand. She's jumpy, but he presumes she's nervous about introducing him to her friends and father. Truthfully, on the drive toward Sjoland, Jukka, too, wondered if he made the right decision—a rash one at that—to celebrate Christmas with virtual strangers. Not that he doesn't know, or at least know of, most people on the islands, especially such an old family as the Ulsson's. He's aware that Uffe and his father and grandfather before him have farmed this area of Sjoland for decades, if not centuries. He also knows Hilda by sight, and knows she used to own a women's clothes shop in the center of Mariehamn. But he has never been inside the house. He's only seen it from the road, standing on a hill above the neatly laid out fields.

Inside, the smell of *glögg* and Christmas food is irresistible, as is the sight of Brit in her slinky outfit. Hilda, too, seems pleased with his presence and very welcoming. Thank goodness he had the foresight to get the flowers.

But then there's Brit's father. Jukka is no longer a teenager meeting the girlfriend's parents, but it feels strange to have such an encounter on Christmas Eve of all days. He straightens his back as Brit leads him by the hand into the living room.

Four men, all holding a small glass of mulled wine, stand in front of a huge Christmas tree. The tree is decorated simply with silver baubles and old-fashioned narrow tinsel, which looks like it's lost some of its silvery shine. But the most striking feature is the live candles, flickering against the darkened windows. The lights are low in the room, making the space look very festive.

Jukka watches Brit go over to the shortest man in the room. 'Dad, let me introduce you to Jukka. He is,' here Brit glances at Jukka and bites her lower lip, 'my friend from the ship.'

Rolf Svensson isn't as short as Jukka first thought, but he has a considerable stoop. His handshake is firm, however, even if his eyes are gray and his frame slight.

'I knew your father,' Rolf says. The words of greeting Jukka was about to utter get caught in his throat. When he doesn't say anything, Brit's father turns toward Mr Ulsson, who is also standing in the small circle. 'You remember him, Uffe, don't you? A real tough guy.'

Jukka can see Brit's face is crumbling, but the situation is saved by Hilda who sweeps into the room with a flourish. 'This is my husband, Uffe.'

The man with gray hair and beard, with a rounded farmer's physique, takes Jukka's hand and pumps it for a long time. His hands are calloused, but his face is warm and friendly.

'Welcome, welcome! And Happy Christmas!'

Before he has time to return the season's good wishes, Hilda touches his arm.

'Why don't you come into the kitchen and meet my daughter, Alicia. She's Brit's best friend from school, did you know that?'

Jukka glances behind him at Brit, who sees his look and decides to follow him.

'Now you do eat everything, don't you? Alicia, would you be an angel and get Jukka a drink?' Hilda is talking non-stop.

Jukka takes a glass of beer, grateful to have escaped the talk about his father.

'Nice to meet you,' Alicia says, looking at Brit. 'I've heard so much about you.'

'As have I!' Hilda says. 'You are a sea captain?' she adds, 'I want you to tell me all about the ships. I use them so often but I have never met one of the captains.'

The older woman leads Jukka back into the living

room, where she dominates the discussions, not letting Brit's father or Uffe Ulsson get a word in. Jukka is grateful and he begins to tell Hilda all about how he took the entrance exams to the Swedish University in Malmö, and how he ended up working on Marie Line.

'Best job I've ever had,' he says.

While is talking, Brit walks back in and stands next to him. He takes in her scent and is momentarily stunned into silence by her intoxicating presence.

Gazing from Brit to Jukka, Hilda squeezes Jukka's arm. 'Please excuse me, I'd better see to the supper.'

Jukka is so grateful to Hilda for rescuing him from talk of his father that he takes her hand and kisses the back of it in the old-fashioned way.

'I can't wait to eat the food you have cooked. It smells delicious.'

Hilda beams at him and leaves them standing in the back of the large lounge.

'What a charmer,' Brit says. Her voice has an edge to it, which Jukka doesn't understand. He puts an arm around her waist and leans close to her. 'I've missed you,' he whispers in her ear.

'Where is that girl?' Hilda says later, while she's checking all the items on the smorgasbord that has been assembled on the kitchen table. She and Alicia decided that it was best to set the cold fish course here, and then serve the hot main course, and the pudding, directly in the dining room. Silently, she's ticking everything off a list in her hand.

Herring in mustard, tick. Herring in curry sauce, tick. Herring with onion and dill, tick. Cold smoked salmon, tick. Gravlax, tick. New potatoes, home cured gherkins, beetroot Rosolli salad, dill sauce, soured cream sauce, two types of rye bread, rye crackers, homemade butter.

'Oh,' Alicia says, looking down at her phone.

'What is it?'

'She's not coming,' Alicia says silently. She's still staring at the screen and Hilda can see tears forming in her eyes.

Hilda folds her list into the pocket of her apron and puts her arm around Alicia's shoulders.

'What does she say?'

But Alicia is already moving away from her, the phone pressed against her ear.

Hilda's just thinking that she needs to remove a place from the table, and wonders how it will all work without Frida there. She was warned by Alicia that the baby may disturb dinner (as if she didn't know that already!), still with eight diners, it would have been perfect with Uffe and Hilda at the ends of the table and three guests either side. Now it's going to be all lopsided. Naturally, Hilda is sorry not to spend Christmas with Frida and her new great-grandchild, but the baby will be too young to appreciate the gifts or the general seasonal merriment, so it's not really that much of a big deal that she isn't coming. Hilda can see Alicia talking in a low tone on the phone. She's holding the handset tightly against her ear, while gesticulating with her other hand.

She's trying to convince Frida to come.

Hilda sighs. She can hear laughter from the lounge.

She picks up her glass and tops it up with white wine. She has a spot by the serving hatch between the kitchen and the lounge where she leaves her glass, so that she can always locate and retrieve it.

She peers out of the opening and sees Jukka telling a story, which is amusing everyone. She's glad to see Rolf and Uffe have stopped talking about the poor boy's parents. She just about rescued the situation. Her impression of Jukka is favorable. She smiles to herself when she thinks how the girls came to her for advice on Brit's new man. She knows she's good at spotting unsuitable boyfriends, not that she ever had much chance to use her skills with her own daughter. She was never allowed to say anything to *her*. When she brought Liam home for the first time, there was no discussion about the relationship not going forward. Alicia was already pregnant by then, so even if she'd had doubts about Liam, there would have been no point in voicing them.

As if he knew she was thinking about him, Liam turns his head toward Hilda and she smiles and raises her glass. Liam has been very subdued all day, and Hilda suspects something has happened between husband and wife. But Alicia, as usual, will tell Hilda what's going on when she's ready, and there is no point in trying to dig it out of her. She just hopes her daughter will see what a good man Liam is and let him look after her. What woman wouldn't be pleased to be married to a surgeon? And to live in London without a care in the world. If she chooses, she doesn't even have to work!

Hilda knows how terrible losing Stefan was and how it knocked them both sideways. As it did Uffe and Hilda, too. Those wounds will never heal, but at the same time they are so young! Hilda wants to tell Liam and Alicia that there is no point in dwelling on what you have lost; you had to look to the future and see what you have.

Just then, a set of headlights appear in the driveway and Hilda shouts to Alicia, 'She's here after all!'

FORTY-NINE

Patrick turns into the Ulsson's drive and parks the car next to a VW Golf. He turns off his lights and stays in the car for a moment. On the passenger seat is a paper bag filled with Christmas presents wrapped up expertly by one of the assistants at the fashionable interior design shop in town. They are beautifully understated, in white paper with wide red ribbons.

There's also the large box containing a magnum of vintage champagne resting on the floor of the car. He wonders if that is overkill. Should he perhaps leave the bottle behind and fetch it later, if he gets a good reception from Alicia?

He gazes up to the house, shining brightly in the dark afternoon light, the downstairs windows decorated with large star lanterns. The freshly fallen snow has formed a blanket over the sloping roof and the landscape. With the large pine draped with white lights, the whole scene looks serene and festive, like a TV advert.

Damn it, be brave.

Hilda will appreciate the champagne, he's sure, so he picks up the box, takes hold of the paper bag, slams the door of his car, and makes his way up to the house.

Alicia cannot believe her eyes. Responding to her mother's call, she moves into the kitchen and watches as Patrick gets out of the car, picking something up from the passenger seat. She has her phone against her ear, still talking to Frida. The baby is crying in the background.

'Can I ring you later?' Alicia says and ends the call.

'Is that who I think it is?' Hilda says, her mouth open, forming an 'o.'

'What the hell does he think he's doing?' Alicia says and hurries to the door.

But Patrick is quicker than she is, and by the time she opens the door, he is already standing there, a wide grin filling his face. He's carrying a bag full of presents and a large box.

'Surprise!' he says.

Alicia stands there, dumbfounded. She cannot speak.

'Can I come in?' Patrick asks. 'It's bloody cold out here.'

'Patrick, what a lovely surprise!' Hilda says. She's standing behind Alicia, who's unable to move or speak. At her mother's words, she turns to scowl at Hilda.

Hilda widens her eyes at her daughter. 'Come now, let the poor man in. He must be freezing.'

Patrick smiles at Hilda and steps past Alicia, who is still holding onto the door handle. Alicia gets a waft of his perfume and the smell of the crisp outside. She tries not to let his rousing presence affect her judgment.

What is he playing at? He must know Liam is here?

'Alicia, close that door before we all catch our death,' Hilda says.

'*God Jul*,' Patrick says and hugs Hilda. He hands her the box he's holding and, when she sees what it is, she exclaims, 'Oh, my goodness. Thank you and Merry Christmas to you too!'

'I'm sorry I've come unannounced, but I thought I'd drop my presents off. I didn't get a chance to do it before today, but I won't keep you.'

With that, he hands the large paper bag to Hilda and turns around.

'Happy Christmas, Alicia.' His voice is soft and he bends down to give her a kiss on the cheek while grabbing the door handle, ready to go back outside.

'Patrick, you can't leave without at least having a drink with us!' Hilda exclaims.

'I couldn't possibly, it's a family occasion,' Patrick says.

Alicia rolls her eyes at him, but he either doesn't see her or ignores her on purpose and, smiling at Hilda, continues, 'If you're sure?'

FIFTY

Liam has been trying to follow the conversation with the help of the newcomer, Jukka, who is translating bits of it for him. They're talking about Brexit, a subject that he wishes Uffe hadn't brought up. But the sea captain is quietly spoken and is constantly glancing toward Brit, who when she arrived, had introduced herself as Alicia's oldest friend.

'I remember you from the wedding,' Liam said, a comment that produced a trickle of laughter from the woman. She was dressed in a red jumpsuit and open-toed shoes with matching red toes peeping out from the flared hems, and was perfectly made up with a deep tan and unnaturally white teeth.

Now, standing on the other side of the room, next to her elderly father, she looks jittery, somehow. Liam thinks it's to do with Jukka, who's standing next to her. They keep exchanging what they think are covert glances, but Liam finds them revealing. He can't quite understand why they don't just stand next to each other, rather than play this cat and mouse game. Seeing the romance unfold in front of him, he feels old.

'They're asking how you feel about Europe,' Jukka says.

But before Liam can answer, they all hear a commotion in the hall. The door from the lounge is open toward the front door, but no one can quite see what is going on.

'Excuse me,' says Uffe and he moves toward the hallway.

When Patrick enters the room, smiling broadly and closely followed by Uffe, Hilda, and Alicia, Liam nearly drops his glass of red wine.

'What would you like to drink? I have some mulled wine, a rather lovely Rioja, or a South African Sauvignon?' says Hilda, fussing over the newest guest.

Patrick chooses the red wine, and goes around the room to shake everyone's hand.

Brit giggles when she says hello to him. 'I've heard so much about you!'

Liam glances at Alicia, who is standing in the doorway to the lounge. She's motionless, as if she's been struck dumb. He moves quickly behind Patrick, nodding to him briefly, and goes over to Alicia. He puts his hand under her elbow.

'You OK?'

'What?' Alicia says, looking at him as if she's just remembered that he is here, in this room with all these people who don't belong here. It's as if all the waifs and strays from the islands have decided to crash Uffe and Hilda's Christmas.

'You're shaking,' he says looking into her face for any signs of a serious health problem.

But Alicia lifts her arm away and says irritably, 'I'm fine. I'm not one of your patients.'

Liam is taken aback by her sudden aggression. Didn't they agree not to spoil Christmas? He wants to say something to that effect, but Patrick is now standing in front of them, gazing at Alicia.

Reluctantly, it seems, Patrick takes his eyes off Alicia and looks in Liam's direction. 'When did you arrive?'

'Merry Christmas to you too,' Liam says and hears the sarcasm in his own voice. He immediately regrets it, and from the corner of his eye he can see Alicia staring at him. With an exasperated expression, no doubt. He doesn't need to turn toward her to know that.

Patrick gives a short, embarrassed laugh. Embarrassment, which is entirely his.

'I'm sorry if I'm spoiling your party. I'll just have this drink and then go.'

Hilda must have heard and understood Patrick's words because she pipes up, 'No, no, Patrick, you stay!'

Patrick gives Liam a wide smile and, switching to Swedish, begins a mock argument with Hilda.

'My mother is saying that we have a spare place because Frida and the baby aren't coming,' Alicia says to Liam.

'What brilliant luck for Patrick,' he replies.

Alicia turns toward him and says in a low voice so that the others can't hear, 'I didn't plan this. I had no idea.'

She moves to the kitchen and leaves Liam standing there, watching the spectacle of the Swede commanding the room. He's telling some story or other about his days as a reporter in Stockholm, in Swedish. Liam doesn't understand a word, something that the man is obviously enjoying immensely, judging by the occasional victorious glances he throws in Liam's direction. The room erupts in laughter as the story comes to an end.

Liam follows Alicia into the kitchen. He can't take any more of Patrick.

In the kitchen Alicia is speaking in low tones to her mother. They are both standing with their back to Liam, bent over the stove. When Hilda spots him, she says, 'Ah, Liam, would you like another drink?'

Alicia says something to her mother in Swedish, and then turns to Liam. 'Can I talk to you for a moment?'

Alicia leads him up the stairs to the attic room, which is pristine, the bed made up with white linen. Once she's closed the door Alicia turns to Liam.

'I'm so sorry,' she says, wringing her hands.

Liam gazes at his wife. He sees a woman he hasn't known in years. Her cheeks are burning, her eyes shining, and her lips are soft and red. She looks extremely attractive. Suddenly, he realizes all this change has happened since the Swede walked into the house.

'But you're glad he's here,' Liam says, sitting down on the bed.

Her heart is beating ten to a dozen. She needs to calm down but doesn't know how. Liam is sitting on the bed, while Alicia paces up and down the small attic room.

'No, I'm *not* glad here's here,' she almost shouts, but seeing Liam's expression, she stops.

'Sit down,' Liam says.

How he can be so calm, Alicia has no idea, but she joins Liam on the bed, a little distance away. Liam turns toward her and lifts her chin, bringing her face to eye level with him.

'Alicia, I know you very well. As much as I'd like to pretend otherwise, I can see how much he means to you. It's far from ideal to have him here for Christmas of all times, but if I can deal with it, so should you. Just make sure your mother sits me as far away from him as possible, eh?'

'Thank you,' Alicia says, now a lot calmer. She removes Liam's hand and squeezes it.

'You're a good man,' she says. She can feel tears well inside her eyelids, but she resists them and gets up instead.

'I'll go down and make sure the table arrangements are OK,' she says and forces a smile.

Liam doesn't say anything but nods to Alicia with a sad expression on his face.

FIFTY-ONE

'Alicia,' Patrick is standing on the second floor landing when, much later, she comes up the stairs. It's dark up there, outside Hilda and Uffe's bedroom, and Alicia doesn't spot him until he is standing in front of her. She's on her way to the loo, forced to come up to Hilda's en-suite bathroom because someone was already using the downstairs cloakroom.

'What are you doing here?'

Patrick doesn't answer her question but presses his lips on her mouth. For a moment she relaxes into his kiss. She's been wanting to be touched by him all evening, resisting the temptation to respond to the pressure of his thigh next to hers under the table. Once he even placed his hand on her arm, but when she looked across the table, she saw Liam's eyes burning into the two of them. Remembering how unfair all of this is on Liam, she now pushes herself away.

'Stop it!'

'Come on, I've missed you!'

'Since yesterday?'

'Yes,' Patrick says and grins. 'I'm in love with you.' He pulls her close to him again and kisses her neck.

Once again, with great effort, because her body just wants to be caressed by this man, Alicia removes herself from Patrick's embrace. She cannot help but return his smile when she says, 'You are terrible. And drunk.'

'It's Christmas Eve!'

'Yes, it is and my husband is downstairs. This is not fair on him.'

Patrick looks down at his hands. 'I know.'

'You shouldn't have come.'

'Perhaps,' Patrick says. He takes Alicia's hands in his. 'I'll get a cab home as soon as Hilda serves coffee. But you have to promise to see me tomorrow.'

'Oh, Patrick, I can't tomorrow. Liam doesn't leave until Boxing Day.'

'I can wait if you'll stay the night this time? The girls aren't back until Sunday so we'll have two glorious days together.'

Alicia nods. She can't imagine spending 48 hours—guilt-free—with Patrick. The prospect just seems too good to be true. She smiles and nods at him.

Patrick gives her another hasty kiss, and before turning toward the staircase, he adds, 'I've saved your present for when we are together again, so don't let me down.'

FIFTY-TWO

There is an atmosphere around the table. Alicia's husband is not saying a word, while Alicia is talking too much. Sitting next to one another, Alicia and Patrick already look like a couple and Liam cannot take his eyes off them. Brit thinks there's going to be an almighty row any second, but then halfway through the main course, Patrick starts to talk about his daughters. He tells them how his eldest, Sara, had meningitis when she was just three years old. He's making a great effort to translate everything into English for Liam's benefit, which Alicia's ex seems to appreciate.

'We nearly lost her,' he says and looks over the table at Liam.

And just like that something passes between the men and Liam replies, 'I'm so sorry to hear that.'

'Don't be. She's fine now but I will never take either of my daughters for granted. Ever.'

'You must miss them, especially now at Christmas

time,' Hilda says and she places a hand on Patrick's forearm resting on the table.

'I do,' but I see them every other weekend, and sometimes more often. 'I'm hoping that once I'm in Stockholm, they will want to stay with me for longer. They're nearly teenagers after all, so I think living in the city will appeal to them.'

Liam stares at Patrick and suddenly he smiles.

'You're leaving the islands?' he asks.

He doesn't notice that Alicia is looking down at her hands, biting her lower lip.

'Yes, I'm going back to the bright lights. To my old job at *Journalen*. I love it on the islands,' Patrick pauses for a moment and glances first at Alicia and then at Hilda, 'but I am a *Stockholmare* at heart.'

'Really, is that so?' Alicia says teasingly, but seems to check herself and quickly adds, 'When are you going?'

'As soon as possible. January 2nd is my first day back.'

A look passes between Patrick and Alicia, and suddenly Brit knows what's going on. He wants her to move to Stockholm with him!

Oh, no, just when we've become friends again!

But Liam doesn't seem to have seen or understood the glances between Alicia and Patrick and he lifts his glass, 'Well, good luck in your new job!'

They all clink their long-stemmed crystal glasses. Rolf and Liam, who are sitting at the far sides of the oval table, get up to ensure they touch each and everyone's drinks.

Brit can almost hear a collective sigh of relief around the table when they are all seated again and Hilda offers more of her excellent vegetable bakes and ham for a second round.

People chat about the food, praising Hilda's cooking, about Stockholm, and the snowy weather, and everyone is in good cheer.

Jukka places a hand over Brit's fingers and whispers, 'I'm so happy to spend Christmas with you.'

Brit gazes at Jukka. His blue eyes are sincere, but can she trust this man? She wants to, with all her heart, but what if he turns out to be another womanizer? Or worse, a predator who thinks touching people up is OK if you're their boss?

She removes her hand from under his grip to take a sip of red wine. It tastes good and since she and her father are staying over at Hilda and Uffe's, and she doesn't need to drive, she can drink as much as she wants. She is stalling, she knows, and wonders if Jukka has noticed. But she is saved by Hilda, who begins to remove plates from the table. Brit and Alicia get up to help. Patrick and Liam, too, rise from their chairs, but Hilda tells them in no uncertain terms to sit back down.

'It's OK, equality hasn't reached Sjoland yet,' Alicia says with a grin, addressing the men.

'Alicia,' her mother reprimands her, but they both laugh. 'They are guests and you are family.' Turning to Brit, who is holding her and Jukka's plates, Hilda says, 'You too, Brit, please stay seated. But Patrick, on second thoughts, perhaps you'd like to open that huge bottle of champagne? I thought we'd have that with the dessert?'

'With pleasure,' he says and follows the women into

the kitchen. Liam, too, gets up, heading toward the bathroom.

Brit's father begins to chat to Uffe about his farm, and Jukka once again takes Brit's hand in his. He has turned in his seat so that he is fully facing her. Brit glances toward her father and Uffe and sees that they are deep in conversation at the other end of the table.

'Is something the matter?' Jukka says. 'Have I upset you for some reason?'

Brit looks hard at Jukka and says, as quietly as she can, 'I had a call from Kerstin.'

Jukka's eyes widen, but he doesn't say anything, so Brit continues, 'She told me about Sia Eklund.'

Jukka drops her hand and leans back in his chair. He runs his fingers over his light brown hair and sighs. He leans toward Brit again and says in a serious tone, while keeping his eyes firmly on hers, 'There was nothing to it. I misread her signals. Besides, she had her own agenda. Did you know she's Kerstin's daughter?'

Brit nods.

When she doesn't say anything, Jukka carries on. 'The company would have sacked me if there'd been any truth to any of it!'

He has raised his voice and Brit is suddenly aware of a hush in the room. Everyone is staring at him. Her father and Uffe, sitting at the table have turned their heads. Alicia and Patrick are standing behind them, also gazing at Brit and Jukka.

Hilda is at the other end of table, carrying a silver tray of champagne glasses, all filled to the brim. She puts it down and in a falsely joyous tone says, 'Bubbles, anyone?'

FIFTY-THREE

On Christmas Day Alicia drives to Mariehamn with Liam. The weather has turned colder, but it's sunny, making the snow-covered fields and the snowy pillows hanging off pine trees and roofs sparkle.

'I'm so sorry about Patrick last night,' Alicia says.

She glances briefly at Liam who is sitting in the passenger seat of her Volvo, wearing his padded coat fully zipped up. Something has happened to the heating in the old car and they can both see their breath vaporize in front of their faces.

'It's OK,' Liam says.

She'd been aware of Liam's discomfort all evening. While they were sitting at the table eating the delicious dishes that Hilda served after the overflowing smorgasbord starter, she'd begun to feel sorry for him. Luckily, she managed to get her mother to seat the two men at opposite ends of the table. But she hadn't realized that this meant Patrick would be next to her. By the time she'd seen where she was sitting, after everybody had found their places, she couldn't ask anyone to move without an explanation. She wonders now if Hilda had done that on purpose? Perhaps her mother thought, if Liam was lost, Patrick was a good second-best? Alicia wouldn't put it past her mother.

She was sure that Liam must have seen Patrick's attempts to touch Alicia all evening. It had been painful, not the joyous family Christmas Alicia had hoped for. And yet, she was happy to sit next to Patrick, and to share the evening with him, and the rest of the people: family, friends, old and new—and Liam.

Liam has hardly said a word to her since Patrick's surprise appearance and their conversation in the attic room. Apart from thanking her for his present, a woolly jumper, and saying goodnight with a brief kiss on her cheek. He had only nodded when Alicia came over to hug him to say thank you for the beautiful gold necklace he had given her.

'It's too much,' she'd whispered into his ear, but he had just smiled and let go of her, almost pushing her away.

Liam stayed behind in the main house, sleeping in the attic room that Hilda had prepared for Frida. Surprisingly, she didn't bat an eyelid when Alicia discreetly asked her if she could find him a bed in the house.

'Of course. You'll be in the sauna cottage, I presume?' Alicia nodded.

'OK, lovely,' Hilda had said, hugging Alicia. She was stunned that her mother didn't make a fuss, or demand an explanation, or even worse, tell her what a brilliant man Liam was and how she was foolish to let him go. This was a lecture she had heard at least dozen times during the last few months. Alicia wonders now if Hilda had seen the way they were together and concluded that their marriage couldn't be saved.

'I used to go out every Christmas Day,' Frida says, hushing the baby, who is crying at full volume. She's speaking English, for Liam's benefit. Something for which Alicia is grateful.

'Really?' Liam says.

'Yes, it's a tradition here. Christmas Eve is for family and Christmas Day for partying,' Alicia says, adding to Frida, 'Do you want me to take her?'

Frida hands Anne Sofie to Alicia and she begins rocking the baby just as she used to do with Stefan. Liam is gazing at the two of them and Alicia can see tears in his eyes. He turns away quickly and asks Frida for a glass of water.

'Oh My God, I haven't even offered you a drink!' the young woman says and goes into the small kitchen. 'What would you like, tea or coffee, or mulled wine?'

'Coffee, please,' both Liam and Alicia say in unison. Liam smiles at Alicia and the baby, who has calmed down and is blinking slowly in her arms. She returns his smile and looks at little Anne Sofie, who has now closed her eyes completely. Gingerly, she steps inside the kitchen and, mouthing to Frida 'She's asleep,' goes to put the baby down in her cot.

When she's tucked the baby in, she comes into the

living room, where Frida and Liam sit facing each other across a low table covered with baby clothes, packets of baby wipes, and one of diapers.

'I'm glad you came over. I'm sorry about last night. She's been so restless for a couple of days now that I didn't think it was a good idea to take her out. Besides, I'm exhausted. I went to bed at six o'clock, just after I put her down last night.' Frida runs her hand across her forehead. Her hair is standing almost upright. The tips have a faint hue of blue, otherwise the color looks almost normal. She's wearing a pair of ripped black tights and a bright red dress.

Alicia sits next to her and gives the girl a hug.

'That's OK. You did the right thing,' she says, letting go of Frida.

She glances toward Liam, who opens his mouth to speak, but Frida speaks first.

'The thing is, I feel a bit of a fraud.

Both Alicia and Liam stare at Frida, who's gazing down at her hands, crossing and uncrossing them.

Alicia touches her arm and asks, 'What do you mean?'

'I'm so sorry!' Frida says and bursts into tears.

Alicia puts her arms around the girl again and looks over at Liam. He widens his eyes in a question, to which Alicia shakes her head.

'What is it? This can't be about last night?' she says to Frida, who has buried her head in Alicia's chest.

'I'm a terrible person. You'll hate me forever,' Frida sobs.

'It's OK, Frida. We already know Stefan isn't Anne Sofie's dad,' Liam says in a matter-of-fact voice.

Frida lifts her head up and stares at him.

'How?' She asks.

Alicia puts her hand up to stop Liam saying anything more. Speaking in Swedish, she says, 'Without telling me, Liam took a hair out of Anne Sofie's head and together with something I had from Stefan, was able to do a DNA test. And it proved conclusively negative.' She lets this information sink in for a moment, and then adds, 'But it doesn't matter to me. I am still Anne Sofie's grandmother.'

Frida is quiet, then she gets up and starts walking up and down the living room, from the bookcase overfilled with old volumes and her mother's trinkets to the window overlooking the apartments next door.

'How long have you known?' Speaking in English, she gazes at Liam and Alicia in turn.

'A few days. Liam told me the day he arrived,' Alicia replies.

Again Frida paces up and down the living room. Liam moves on his seat and opens his mouth, but Frida stops him once more. 'And when were you going to tell me?'

'Today. Now,' Liam replies.

Frida nods.

'Sit down, Frida. Can I ask why you let us believe Stefan was Anne Sofie's dad?' Alicia says as gently as she can.

Frida lowers herself on the sofa and blows air out of her mouth.

'We were in love. So much in love.' She looks pleadingly at Alicia.

'I know,' she says.

Liam gets up. Looking at both Alicia and Frida, he says, 'Do you want me to wait in the car?'

'What?' Alicia says.

'No, Liam, you have a right to know what happened,' Frida says decisively in English.

'Stefan and I met just as I told you in Mariehamn and then again in Brighton when I was there on a language course. But we didn't do anything. There was nowhere, to, you know,' here Frida looks at Liam and then Alicia. 'Besides, we wanted to wait.'

Alicia puts her hand on Frida's and squeezes it.

'So who?'

'Who's Anne Sofie's father?'

'Yes,' Alicia says.

'Daniel,' the girl says so quietly that Alicia and Liam have to lean forward to hear her.

'It was right after Stefan's accident. I was so sad, and he was there and we got very drunk one night and I don't even remember much of it. I felt so awful afterwards. I'd been unfaithful to Stefan with Daniel of all people, and then I found out I was pregnant. Well, I kept thinking and hoping it would be Stefan's. But, of course, it couldn't have been. I'm such a fool.'

'Did Daniel know, before he perished?'

Frida nods. She's not looking at either Alicia or Liam.

There is an awkward silence, which is interrupted by a baby crying.

Frida leaves the room and they hear her talking softly to Anne Sofie, who gurgles in reply. Alicia looks at Liam.

'Do you think we should leave her to it?' Liam says and gets up.

Alicia nods and hands the car keys to Liam, 'You go on, I'll just say goodbye to Frida.'

FIFTY-FOUR

'She lied to us. Just as,' Liam says, but Alicia stops him.

'Yes, I was there, I heard her. What are you going to say now, "I told you so?"'

Liam takes a deep breath and Alicia can see his chest rise and fall next to her in the car, but he doesn't reply to her. They are driving back along the empty streets, with just the occasional vehicle coming in the other direction in the center of town.

'You'll have to tell Uffe and Hilda,' Liam says after a while. They've just crossed over the swing bridge in Sjoland and are nearing Alicia's home.

Hilda is in the kitchen, preparing another feast for the evening. Uffe is at the sink, peeling potatoes. His back is to them when Alicia and Liam step into the room. It's warm inside, with candles flickering on the table in a wooden red and white candelabra.

'There they are!' Hilda exclaims, making Uffe turn around. He lifts his wet hands out of the sink and says, 'More food to be prepared.' He's grinning widely and nods toward Hilda. 'Mind you, we have enough to last till next Christmas!'

'Nonsense,' Hilda replies and smacks Uffe's back with a tea towel.

'Can we do anything to help?' Alicia asks, but Hilda says, 'No, we're not going to eat until much later. How was Frida and the little baby?' she adds.

'Fine,' Alicia says.

'Have you had anything to eat?' Hilda asks next, a question that makes Alicia and Liam, after she's translated what her mother has said, smile.

'No.'

'Oh, in that case, let's all have some coffee. I've got some wonderful Karelian pies I bought from the market and cinnamon buns. And there are Christmas stars.'

After the table is set with the rye-crust rice-filled pies, sweet pastries, and cinnamon buns, and everyone has eaten far too much again, Alicia says, 'Mom and Uffe, we have something to tell you.'

Her serious tone stops Hilda in her tracks. She puts down her cup of coffee and gazes at her daughter.

'I think I know what's coming,' she says, glancing sideways at Liam.

'We have two things to tell you,' Alicia says. She looks at Liam, who is sitting next to her, and says to him in English, 'I'll tell them, and then I'll translate. OK?'

Liam nods and Alicia continues, 'Liam did a DNA test on the baby.'

Both Uffe and Hilda gasp. Her mother puts a hand to her mouth. 'She's not ours!' she exclaims.

'Now, now, don't jump to conclusions,' Uffe says, patting Hilda's hand.

But she takes no notice of her husband and says instead, 'I knew it, I knew it all along!'

'Mom, yes, you are right. But that doesn't mean that Frida didn't love Stefan. And Stefan most certainly was in love with her.'

Alicia tells Hilda and Uffe everything Frida has told them. About how she slept with Daniel, Stefan's friend, the Romanian boy who'd worked on Uffe's farm and so tragically died last summer.

Then she adds, 'I also found out who Frida's father is.'

FIFTY-FIVE

'You know that she is a vindictive woman?' Jukka says.

'Yes, but there must have been something to it. And this Sia, I mean she can't have been very old,' Brit replies.

Jukka sighs. 'Yes, I admit, I was stupid and it was totally wrong of me in that sense. She was coming onto me and I thought she wanted it.'

'When you say "it", what do you mean exactly? What happened?' Brit now demands.

They are sitting in Brit's apartment, on one of the light-colored sofas. The night before, Jukka had left Hilda and Uffe's place a few moments after they'd toasted the season with Patrick's expensive champagne. Jukka wasn't drinking because he was on call, and because he was driving back home after the festivities. He also didn't take any presents, something he felt pretty bad about, and he'd decided to leave before the traditional exchange of gifts.

'We had sex, but only once.'

'As if that would make any of it better!'

'But it was two years ago! And it has nothing to do with you.'

Brit sighs. Jukka is right, of course. His previous sexual escapades have nothing to do with her. If she pursues this, she could come across as needy and spoil her chances with Jukka altogether. They've only had sex once and are by no means an item. Except, he agreed to come and spend Christmas with her best friend's family—and meet her father. So she must mean something more to him than just what happened in Solbacken two days ago?

'Look,' Jukka takes her hands in his. 'I am falling for you. When I was with Sia, it was to do with my wife, my ex, and I wasn't myself.'

Jukka lets go of Brit and leans back on the sofa.

'I don't know what to tell you, except that it won't happen again,' he says, looking out across the wintry view out of his window.

'Really?' Brit bites her lip after she's made the sarcastic comment.

Stop being so needy!

'Yes, really. Why do you think it took me so long to ask you for a drink?'

Now Brit thinks back to their last shift together on MS *Sabrina*. She was confused about his behavior. He *was* blowing hot and cold and she couldn't understand what he was playing at. She looks at him, sitting upright on the sofa next to her. His hands are knitted together, resting on his thighs. He's wearing a striped shirt but the strong muscles in his arms are flexed and showing underneath the clothing.

Why does he have to be so good-looking?

Brit wants to sit across his lap and have those strong arms around her waist. She wants to see how quickly she can make him hard. She gazes down at her outfit. Luckily, when Jukka phoned and asked if he could come over and talk to her just after midday, just as she was getting ready to go and spend the Christmas Day evening with her dad, she'd had time to change into a slinky black dress and some sexy underwear.

A girl can never be too prepared.

But what if he is a complete rat, and this is the way he gets over the women he plays?

'You look very nice, by the way. I've been wanting to take you in my arms all night.'

Brit leans over and brings her lips toward Jukka. He takes hold of her waist and pulls her onto his lap. They start kissing and tumble onto the sofa.

FIFTY-SIX

'What about the two of you?' Hilda asks.

Liam has understood her question, Hilda thinks. He exchanges a look with her daughter and immediately looks down at his empty coffee cup on the table. And Hilda understands. Alicia has decided to leave him. Of course, Hilda suspected that already. Seeing Alicia with Patrick yesterday confirmed her suspicions about those two too.

'Mom, I'm sorry, but Liam is leaving tomorrow and we've decided to separate.'

No one says anything. Uffe is looking out into the snow-covered fields across the window at the far end of the kitchen. He hasn't said a word while Alicia has been speaking, as if none of it has anything to do with him. Mostly, he appears embarrassed. As usual, he's leaving everything to her.

I bet he wishes he was hiding in his study now.

'I'm sorry to hear that,' Hilda says in English and

then, addressing her daughter in Swedish, 'I guess you're going to go swanning off to Stockholm with Patrick?'

That gets everyone's attention, even Uffe is back in the room.

'What did you say?' he asks.

'Mom!' Alicia says and gets up. Like a teenager, she runs out of the room and up the stairs.

Liam is staring at Hilda and she suspects that once again, Liam has managed to understand Swedish.

'Go after her,' Hilda says and Liam rushes toward the staircase.

'What?' Hilda exclaims when she sees Uffe's expression. 'It's about time she made up her mind which one of them she wants,' she says.

'A bit cruel, don't you think?' Uffe says quietly.

Hilda sighs. He's probably right, but what is she supposed to think, or do? After all the surprises she's had to contend with today, and in the last year, she just wants to get back to normal.

'She was always the same as a girl. Couldn't make a decision to save her life,' she says and starts clearing the table.

FIFTY-SEVEN

U p on the third floor of the house, Liam sees that the door to the attic room is shut. He stands outside for a moment, listening to any sounds coming from inside, but since it all seems completely still in there, he gives the door a gentle knock.

'Yes?' he hears Alicia say.

'It's me,' Liam replies.

When there's nothing more from Alicia, Liam opens the door.

Alicia is sitting on the bed, with a tissue in her hand. She looks vulnerable in her loose blue jeans and thin, red cashmere jumper, which has gold glitter at the wrists and along the high collar. He thinks she must have lost weight again since he last visited. He hasn't noticed it on this trip before, but seeing her now, with her back resting against the wall with her legs pulled up and hands wrapped around her knees, she looks thin and fragile.

Liam sits on the far edge of the bed. 'You OK?'

Alicia nods.

'It's been quite a Christmas,' Liam says.

Alicia lifts her eyes up at him and gives him a sad smile.

'Yes.'

'Not quite how you'd planned it?'

Alicia laughs. A short snort, really, but Liam takes it as a good sign.

'Can I ask you something?'

'It's OK, Liam. I'm not going to move to Stockholm with him,' Alicia says. She's looking at him, but now Liam doesn't know what to say.

'But our marriage is over,' Alicia adds.

'OK,' Liam says. 'OK,' he repeats, and then, knowing he shouldn't but unable to help himself, he asks, 'So you and him aren't an item?'

Alicia gazes at Liam for a long time, and he doesn't know what she is thinking. He's dying to say something but is certain that he has already said too much. Or that whatever he says now will spoil it for him forever.

'Liam, it really isn't any of your business. I'm truly sorry, but I know that I haven't felt what I used to feel for you for some years now. Stefan, well, Stefan in a way was the catalyst. I don't love you anymore. And if there is someone else, that's for me to tell you. If and when I wish to share that information. You lost the right to know when you decided to break our marriage vows.'

'And Frida and Anne Sofie?' Liam says.

'I don't know about that. I'll see how it all goes. I love that little baby girl and her mother more than I thought I could love anyone new, and I can't just turn that love off.

You do understand that, don't you?' Alicia says. Now there are tears in her eyes.

'I'm so sorry, I thought I was doing the right thing with the test. I thought you'd want to know. I've been such a fool!' Liam shuffles over to where Alicia is sitting at the other end of the bed. He lays a hand over Alicia's wrist, and adds, 'Can you forgive me?'

'Yes, Liam, I do know you were just thinking of what the best thing for everyone would be. Besides, it doesn't much matter now anyway. It seems the truth had been torturing Frida too, so she would have told me sooner or later. It was almost better coming from you. At least I was prepared when she told me.'

'All the same, I'm so sorry,' Liam says.

Alicia moves off the bed and kneels in front of Liam. She puts her arms around him.

'Let's try to be friends, eh?'

Liam nods inside Alicia's embrace. Her scent of roses and jasmine, so feminine and so familiar, is pulling at his heart and he feels tears—he never cries!—pricking his eyes.

Liam gently pushes Alicia away and says, 'I better pack before the re-run of food and drink fest tonight. I was quite worse for wear last night.'

She gives him a last squeeze and steps off the bed. At the door, Alicia stops and turns around, 'You are a kind man. I'm not saying anything to the contrary, you know that, don't you?' And with those words Alicia, his lovely Scandinavian wife, walks out of his life forever.

FIFTY-EIGHT

On Boxing Day, Alicia gets a message from Patrick. He's been unusually quiet since they parted under the full gaze of everyone on Christmas Eve, and Alicia hasn't wanted to be the first to contact him, even though they decided to spend the rest of the holidays together. She doesn't know what she's going to tell him.

Are you coming over?

Alicia regards the text and smiles. What is she going to do?

Let's have coffee in town. Bagarstugan?

Half an hour later, when Alicia steps into the small coffee place, busy with shoppers who are in the little town for post-Christmas bargains. Patrick is in the back of the rammed room, at a small table with two chairs on either side.

'I got you a cappuccino,' he says. He gets up to give her a kiss and she cannot resist it, but lets his lips touch hers for far longer than is wise in front of all these people.

There is bound to be someone that either she, or more likely, Patrick, knows. Or someone who recognizes one of them. Apart from Patrick's dubious reputation as the former son-in-law of the richest man on the islands, both their images are plastered over *Ålandsbladet* and its internet edition, which is read by about three times as many people as the paper version.

'How are you?' Patrick leans over and now, as if the kiss wasn't enough for the many eyes Alicia feels sure are boring into her back, he takes Alicia's hands in his.

'I'm fine,' she replies, and adds in a low voice, 'Isn't this a bit too public?'

'Your choice,' Patrick says and leans back in his chair. He's grinning from ear to ear.

'You're impossible. Let me take a couple of sips and we'll go over to yours.'

'Suits me,' Patrick says and finishes his black coffee in one gulp.

'I can't leave the islands. Not now. Frida and Anne Sofie, my mother and Uffe, and now Brit, are here,' Alicia says. They are sitting opposite each other at Patrick's white table, drinking wine.

'But things have changed, haven't they?'

'If you mean that I am no longer Anne Sofie's grandmother and that Dudnikov is her grandfather and that Frida is fine, financially speaking, yes. But I still love that little girl. And Frida, of course. I can't turn my feelings off just like that.'

'No, neither can I, and that is just what you've been

asking me to do for these past four months,' Patrick doesn't sound annoyed, even though Alicia can see that she has been indecisive. Not being able to choose between the two men, and her two lives, in London and on the islands, has left both in limbo.

'I've been very confused, I'm sorry,' Alicia says.

She gazes at Patrick who is wearing a white T-shirt as usual, revealing his strong chest and arms. His blond hair has grown longer, and his chin is clean shaven, and for once, there are no shaving cuts. Alicia wants to joke about the lack of scars, but it doesn't seem right to do that now.

Patrick nods slowly.

'The thing is, while you've not been able to decide, I've had to think for myself. And I want to do something more than report on stolen flower pots and delayed ferries.' Patrick looks intently at Alicia.

'At the *Journalen* I can make a difference. Report and investigate real issues, real stories.'

Alicia sighs. She, too, is bored with *Ålandsbladet.* She craves a good story, a corruption case or just a good, old-fashioned financial crisis.

'Stockholm isn't that far! You can get over to Mariehamn in four hours,' Patrick says and he grabs Alicia's' hands.

'That's right, it isn't that far. We can see each other almost every weekend. I can come over to you, or you come over here. Surely you'll have to do that for the girls anyway?'

Patrick throws his arms up in the air.

'You are the most frustrating woman I've ever met!' Biting the inside of his cheek and keeping his eyes firmly on Alicia, he continues, 'The girls will come to me in Stockholm every other weekend. I'll only be coming over here during the summer. Besides, the job at *Journalen* is pretty full-on.'

'Mia has agreed to this?'

Now Patrick looks annoyed, 'Yes, anything to get me off these golden islands.'

She shouldn't have mentioned Mia, Alicia thinks.

But then Patrick's face softens, 'I didn't tell you this before, because I didn't want to make you mad. Or to think that I was taking you for granted,' Patrick pauses for a moment to laugh, 'which is such a joke!'

'What?' Alicia asks, suddenly interested in spite of herself.

'I know one of the guys working on *Dagens Finans* and he says there's a post open there. You know, it's a very similar paper to the *Financial Times*. It's just a maternity cover for a year, or maybe only six months, if you wish, but my mate says you'll definitely get it if you apply.'

Alicia is staring at Patrick. Suddenly she imagines herself working in Stockholm, writing relevant stories, not just about lost pets or shop opening times.

She could be going out to lunches with Patrick, not having to worry about who will see them or what stories will get back to her mother and Uffe. And she would still be able to come and see everyone here in Åland every weekend if she wanted to. Or at least every other weekend, when Patrick has her daughters over. And it could just be a trial. Six months, a year, to see how it goes?

'If you don't like me or Stockholm after a year, you

can just move back to the islands,' Patrick says as if he's read her mind.

He's giving her his most charming smile.

Why not? I can do what I want for the first time in my life.

'OK, you win, if I get that job, I'll try Stockholm out for six months,' Alicia says and grins at Patrick.

'Really?' he says and jumps up from his chair. In a second, he's got his arms around Alicia and he's kissing her.

'I can't believe I've finally got you!'

EPILOGUE

In late January, Patrick moves into his new penthouse property. The two-bedroom apartment overlooks Kungsholmen island across the Riddar-fjärden channel. He is in his favorite part of town, Söder. His daughters have already visited him for one weekend and they love that they can walk into the most fashionable shops and cafés in the trendy part of town. His eldest, Sara, had her hair cut into a short pixie, and spent Saturday morning in the area's popular secondhand shops. Both his daughters are into sustainability and avid followers of Greta Thunberg, much to their mother's annoyance.

On the Sunday morning, after he's handed Sara and Frederica back to Mia, at the Marie Line ferry port, Patrick looks at the pretty pale yellow and red brick houses, with their jagged roofs topped with layers of snow, on the other side of the water from his new apartment. The sea is iced over, with a narrow shipping lane cutting it in half. A small tug boat is making its way through the channel. The sun is out and the view is making Patrick feel better about the sudden emptiness of the apartment. Unlike in Mariehamn, where the view was of open sea, void of any signs of habitation, and with only the twice-daily ferry traffic, Patrick can feel the pulsating life of a city, even if he can't make out the people on the streets. He cannot wait to share this view and show the city off to Alicia. She's coming over on Wednesday for an interview, which Patrick has been reliably informed is just a formality, with *Dagens Finans.* Initially, Alicia will work for the paper for six months, starting in February, but she has insisted that she will look for a rental as soon as possible. Patrick is confident that once she's shared his bed for a few weeks, she will forget about finding her own place. Besides, getting a rental in Stockholm is notoriously difficult. But Patrick has decided not to push her. They have agreed that her stay in Stockholm, and particularly with him, is strictly a temporary measure, and that's fine with Patrick—for now.

Alicia is packing up the sauna cottage. She's decided to stay in Stockholm with Patrick for the week, coming back to the islands on the last ferry on Sunday. Irrespective of how the interview with Swedish newspaper goes, she will move in with Patrick on the first Monday in February. In the meantime, Hilda and Alicia have decided to shut up the cottage for winter. She was surprised at how well her mother took the news of her plans.

'You are young,' Hilda said, wiping a tear from the

corner of her eye. 'And you must start living your life again. Stockholm is only a skip and a hop away.'

Alicia hugged her mother and promised she would come and see her every other weekend, when Patrick's daughters were in town.

'You mustn't worry about me,' Hilda says, pulling away from her daughter's embrace. 'Surely you will need to get to know the girls if your relationship with Patrick is serious?'

Alicia looked down at her hands. This was one issue she hadn't dared think about. Having only ever had a son, she has no idea how to deal with pre-teen girls. Plus, she knows Mia isn't exactly thrilled about Alicia and Patrick's plans.

That morning, as she looks at her scarce possessions, which fit into one suitcase and two large IKEA bags, one of which is filled with Hilda's linen used in the cottage, she thinks back to the past six months in this small space. So much has happened that she would never forget. She's found out that she has strengths that she never thought she possessed, and that she has the ability to love again. Thinking of love, the image of little Anne Sofie comes to her mind. Frida, too, understood and was glad about Alicia's decision. Much like Hilda, she mentioned the short distance between the Swedish capital and Mariehamn.

'You do know that some people commute each week back and forth?' Frida said and laughed. 'So you can come and see your granddaughter whenever the fancy takes you.' The young mother had handed Alicia the baby as soon as she stepped inside the door, and when

Alicia heard Frida call Anne Sofie her granddaughter, tears pooled in eyes, but she wiped them away and smiled.

'I know,' she said.

'But I have to say, you're a bit of a dark horse! Patrick Hilden, no less.'

At those words, Alicia blushed. She turned away from Frida and sat down with the baby, who was wriggling to get out of her grasp. Lately, all she wanted to do was stand up on her knees, and as Alicia held Anne Sofie by her little hands, the girl pushed herself up and gave a self-satisfied giggle.

'She is so lovely, I will miss her terribly!'

Frida looked down at Alicia and came to sit next to her on the sofa. She wrapped her hands around Alicia and her daughter, who immediately began to protest. Both Alicia and Frida laughed, which produced a fresh gurgle from the baby.

'You'll see her almost as often as before. And I will come and check out Patrick's posh pad in Stockholm too. You never know, once this little one is a bit older, I might move there myself!' Frida said and bent down to give the top of Anne Sofie's head a kiss.

Alicia gazed at the young woman who had become such a good mother. The apartment, as always, was in a chaotic state, but Frida's disorganization didn't seem to affect the baby's or her own well-being. With the money Frida had access to, which couldn't, as far as Alicia understood, be traced to Dudnikov, and therefore would never be under investigation, both she and her daughter were guaranteed a safe and prosperous future. Alicia didn't want to ask Frida what she was planning to do with all the money, but she was glad to hear the young woman was thinking about the future.

The future, Alicia thinks to herself. What will it hold for any of them? All she knows is that she loves Patrick and she wants to be with him. If they can't stand to live with each other, so be it. Now it feels good to have a nice place to stay in Stockholm (Patrick's descriptions and the photos he's sent her are amazing), with the possibility of a prestigious job to boot.

At that moment, her phone pings and she sees it's a message from Liam.

Good luck with your job interview. xx

She smiles at the message and pens a 'Thank you' reply. Typical of Liam not to know when the interview is, but she's glad that he's happy for her. He always wanted her to build up her career again.

Liam and Alicia have agreed to put the house in Crouch End on the market in the spring, and perhaps by then Alicia will know whether Stockholm and living with Patrick suit her, and him. Her share of the proceeds from the house would buy a comfortable apartment either in Sweden or on the islands, and if the job in Stockholm works out, and is made permanent, she might even be able to take out a loan to get a bigger, or better located place. But these are all decisions she will make later, much later. Now she needs to finish sorting out the cottage. Hilda has promised a celebration brunch at the main house, after which she will drive Alicia to Mariehamn.

Brit hasn't told Alicia she will be at the ferry port to wave her goodbye. The two friends have already had their farewell dinner in town, after which they went to Brit's apartment where Alicia stayed the night and they talked and talked through most of it. Brit will miss Alicia, especially now that they have only recently rekindled their friendship, but as Alicia pointed out, they will see each other in Stockholm almost as often as they now do on the islands.

It's a bitterly cold day, with no sun and gray skies giving only a faint light to the early afternoon. Brit is waiting outside the terminal building, keeping an eye out for Hilda's red BMW. A few other passengers are dropped off outside the double doors; Brit knows the 12:45 Sunday sailing to Stockholm is a popular one with weekly commuters to the city. Brit herself will step onboard MS *Sabrina* a couple of hours later that same afternoon. She's still sharing her shifts with Jukka, although they haven't yet made their relationship official with Marie Line. Brit smiles when she thinks about Jukka that morning. She stayed over in his apartment in Solbacken and he brought her breakfast in bed. Afterward they made love and he told her that he loved her.

Is it possible to be this happy? Surely something will go wrong soon?

As Hilda's car comes into view, it takes just minutes for it to stop in front of Brit. Hilda has always driven too fast, but in this icy weather, her speeding looks positively dangerous.

'I couldn't let you go without another hug,' Brit says to Alicia, who, looking a little pale, steps out of the low-slung sports car.

'We just about made it in one piece,' Alicia says to Brit under her breath, and laughs.

'Brit, what a lovely surprise,' Hilda says, locking the car remotely with a flourish.

Alicia is wearing her padded coat and a pair of shiny boots. With the color returning to her cheeks, she looks positively beaming. Brit hugs her and says, 'Let me know how the interview goes. I'll be in Stockholm in two days' time, if you have time for a quick drink?'

'That would be lovely,' Alicia says and smiles.

'Come on, let's get you checked in,' Hilda says, to which Alicia rolls her eyes and Brit raises her eyebrows. There's more than half an hour until sailing, so there's plenty of time.

'I've got to get going,' Brit says and puts her arms around Alicia one more time. 'I've got to pack and change before work, but promise to let me know as soon as you know about the job? Ring me or message whenever, yes?'

'Ok,' Alicia replies and Brit can see there are tears in her eyes. She squeezes her friend one more time and says, 'We'll see each other in a couple of days, so this isn't exactly goodbye!'

Hilda is immensely proud of her daughter. She's beautiful and strong. As she watches her speak with the check-in clerk inside the ferry terminal, she can see and hear how assured she is. Patrick, it seems, has been able to win her over, something which surprised Hilda at first, and Uffe. Of course, both of them knew something had been going on with those two ever since the Midsummer party at the Eriksson's house last summer. It made both of them laugh. How ignorant the youngsters think old people are.

'It's as if we've never been in love,' Hilda said to Uffe, who just shook his head and gave a small chuckle.

Hilda herself cannot even remember the number of times she's been infatuated with a man. What's more it still keeps happening, even now. She knows Uffe notices her little affairs of the heart, which she never (not lately, at least) does anything about.

Hilda thinks the new generations are far too serious about life. It's short, so you might as well enjoy it as much as you can. That's her motto, and now her earnest daughter seems to have understood this too. Of course, she's sad to see her leave the islands, but Alicia has been living in London all these years, a place much farther afield, with another language to cope with too. And Hilda just loves Stockholm, so she's looking forward to visiting Alicia as often as possible.

'This is me, I think I'll go through,' Alicia now says. She's standing in front of Hilda with her boarding documents in her hand. Her eyes are full of tears, which makes Hilda fill up too. She puts her arms around her daughter.

'I love you, darling, and I think you are making the right decision,' Hilda says, trying to keep her voice level. 'It's only across the water,' Hilda adds, letting go of Alicia.

'So it is,' her daughter replies and turning to go, adds, 'I love you too, mom.'

THE DAY WE MET

Would you like find out how it all started? The Day We Met is a prequel story to *Love on the Island* -series.

This short story is only available free to members of my Readers' Group.

Go to *helenahalme.com* to get your free story today!

ABOUT THE AUTHOR

Helena Halme grew up in Tampere, central Finland, and moved to the UK via Stockholm and Helsinki at the age of 22. She is a former BBC journalist and has also worked as a magazine editor, a bookseller and, until recently, ran a Finnish/British cultural association in London.

Since gaining an MA in Creative Writing at Bath Spa University, Helena has published ten fiction titles, including six in *The Nordic Heart* Romance Series.

Helena lives in North London with her ex-Navy husband. She loves Nordic Noir and sings along to Abba songs when no one is around.

You can read Helena's blog at www.helenahalme.com, where you can also sign up for her *Readers' Group* and receive an exclusive, free short story, *The Day We Met*.

Find Helena Halme online
www.helenahalme.com
hello@helenahalme.com

ALSO BY HELENA HALME

The Nordic Heart Romance Series:

The Young Heart (Prequel)

The English Heart (Book 1)

The Faithful Heart (Book 2)

The Good Heart (Book 3)

The True Heart (Book 4)

The Nordic Heart Books 1-4

The Christmas Heart (Book 5)

Love on the Island Series:

The Island Affair (Book 1)

An Island Christmas (Book 2)

The Island Daughter (Book 3)

Coffee and Vodka: A Nordic family drama

The Red King in Helsinki: Lies, Spies and Gymnastics

A NOTE FROM THE AUTHOR

I hope you enjoyed *An Island Christmas!*

You may have heard authors talk about reviews and how important reader reviews are for the success of the title. So if you liked this story, I'd be hugely grateful if could write a review either for your favorite online store, or on Goodreads.

Thank you.

ACKNOWLEDGMENTS

As always, I couldn't have written a word without the solid support and encouragement from a whole army of people.

Firstly, my long-suffering Englishman, who puts up with all the highs and lows of a writer's life.

During the publication process of this novel, I lost my Dad, and I couldn't have coped with all the sadness and grief without my brave sister, Anne, and my beautiful and supportive children. Markus and Monika, you are complete stars and I cannot imagine how I managed to be gifted with two such wonderful people.

Talking of gifts, my hugely talented daughter-in-law, Rebecca, has given me the ultimate prize, a beautiful granddaughter. This little girl has been, and continues to be, a tonic to me in my grief.

I must also mention a group of other indie writers that I count as my best friends. Being able to vent my frustrations of life, writing and publishing as well as sharing my achievements with these wonderful women is a privilege.

Thank you Jessica Bell, Carol Cooper, Jane Davis, Jane Dixon-Smith, Lorna Fergusson, Clare Flynn, Jean Gill, Linda Gillard, Karen Inglis, Jill Marsh, Amie McCracken, Laura Morelli, Roz Morris, Alison Morton, Liza Perrat, and Debbie Young. You are all in my heart.

Last, but not at all least, I am eternally grateful to my talented team. My editor, Dorothy Stannard, and my cover designer, Jessica Bell, proved to me once again how much I rely on your support and work.